The Sky Was Always Underground

A Lyric Memoir Of Appalachia

Jonathan Graham

CATAMOUNT
PRESS

an imprint of Sunbury Press, Inc.
Mechanicsburg, PA USA

an imprint of Sunbury Press, Inc.
Mechanicsburg, PA USA

For information about special discounts for bulk purchases, please contact Sunbury Press Orders Dept. at (855) 338-8359 or orders@sunburypress.com.

To request one of our authors for speaking engagements or book signings, please contact Sunbury Press Publicity Dept. at publicity@sunburypress.com.

FIRST CATAMOUNT PRESS EDITION: January 2024

Set in Adobe Garamond | Interior design by Crystal Devine | Cover by Lawrence Knorr | Edited by Lawrence Knorr.

Publisher's Cataloging-in-Publication Data
Names: Graham, Jonathan, author.
Title: The sky was always underground : a lyric memoir of Appalachia / Jonathan Graham.
Description: First trade paperback edition. | Mechanicsburg, PA : Catamount Press, 2024.
Summary: Willow Grove Mine cries out for a secret passage to air in a poem in this hybrid memoir that chronicles an enclave of immigrant Slovak coal miners as they struggle in the aftermath of an explosion that claimed 72 lives in Southeastern Ohio in the mid-20 th century.
Identifiers: ISBN : 979-8-88819-168-2 (paperback) | ISBN : 979-8-88819-169-9 (ePub).
Subjects: BIOGRAPHY & AUTOBIOGRAPHY / Cultural, Ethnic & Regional | FICTION / Small Town & Rural | POETRY / America / General.

Product of the United States of America
0 1 1 2 3 5 8 13 21 34 55

For the Love of Books!

*For my father, a coal miner who worked at Willow Grove Mine
in Belmont County, Ohio. His father and two uncles
also worked there, as did my mother's father.*

*For Vera Troyanovich, my grandmother,
who taught me the important things.*

*For the canary, the sacrificial singer in the mines that saved
countless lives by warning of the silent killers poisoning the air:
whitedamp, blackdamp, firedamp and afterdamp.*

Contents

IV.

Acknowledgments

The author wishes to thank the editors of journals and venues in which versions of these poems and stories have appeared.

I Thought I Heard a Cardinal Sing: Ohio's Appalachian Voices Anthology 2022: "End of the Road;" "A Broken Song for the Willow Grove Mine Disaster;" "Painting the Mountain."

Common Threads: Ohio Poetry Assoc Annual Journal of Work 2021: "Springhouse."

Under The Blossom That Hangs On The Bough: 2020 Edith Chase Symposium Anthology: "Applewood, Butterflies and Summer Rain."

Everything Waits (Poetry Collection, Cornerstone Press 2023): "Applewood, Butterflies and Summer Rain;" "Rolling on Red Dog;" "Springhouse;" "Sitting in the Same Dark;" "The Widow Maker;" "This Light of Home;" "End of the Road."

Open Earth Foundation's Open Earth III 2023: "Appalachia Healing."

———

Gratitude to the two influential poets I found my way to know: James Dickey, who instructed me formally at the University of South Carolina, and Maj Ragain, of Kent State University, who taught me informally through the exchange of poems and letters.

Thanks to Jamie DeMonte, Gregory Vasse, Mary Greer, Annie Dawid, Carol D. Guerrero-Murphy, Kathy Blair Bergstrom, and Lee Elliott for their help with the manuscript.

Preface

On the morning of March 16, 1940, light snow cloaked the Appalachian foothills in Southeastern Ohio. My grandfathers, Russell Graham and Mike Troyanovich, walked out of Willow Grove Mine at daybreak after working the hoot owl shift. Years later they would recall how quiet the morning was, how snow muffled the sound of their voices, and how sunlight dazzled branches of apple trees limned in white on the hill above Willow Grove. They passed my two uncles, Johnny Sklenica and Cecil Grimes, amongst the scores of men walking into the mine to begin their day turn. At 11 A.M., an explosion blew steel doors off their hinges.

Seventy-two miners died, including both my uncles and five men from Midway, my hometown of forty houses where every man was a coal miner, and all but two, my father and one other, were Czechoslovakian immigrants. Word got out. Schools closed early. Wives and families rushed to the mine. The suddenness rendered even the canaries useless. The earth shook for miles. The mine caved in—air in the 22 South tunnel faint in the afterdamp. Afterward, most survivors recovered, but it took years, more than some had in front of them. A few, mostly wives and parents of the fallen, relived the explosion day after day. *The Sky Was Always Underground* tells the story of growing up in the aftermath of Willow Grove.

Jon Graham

I.

In Faint Canary Air

Our life is twofold; Sleep hath its own world,
A boundary between the things misnamed
        Death and existence: Sleep hath its own world,
And a wide realm of wild reality . . .
                —George Gordon Byron, *The Dream*

Father, you labor with syncopated breath
from the tomb of Willow Grove, embalmed
with black smoke and charred remains
of a subterranean explosion in coal.

On the eve of the blood moon,
air still faint in the mineshaft moves in and out—
the sound of a breathing ghost in the afterdamp
let in below me from a tunnel dug beneath my room.

Out of faint canary air, you come to me after a half-century of moons,
looking for a place closer to the road between Powhatan and Fairpoint.

I take your pulse,
find only a miner's
dream for immortality
as we walk the road
through shadows on snow and soot,
together—father and son,
circular and sentient,
promises lived,
heaven and earth reunited.

Air still faint in the tunnel,
the canary flutters in his cage.

The moon phases away,
a bituminous stone in a dark sky.

Painting the Mountain

In the selfless light
of morning,
we sat side by side
painting the mountain.
Just us two
on Christmas day,
facing the Appalachian
foothills, sunlight
above the cliffside
in our eyes.

Coal country
watercolorist by day,
classical violinist by night,
Mother, you made art easy,
in-your-blood right.
When I tried to paint
details of every tree
on the mountain
onto my canvas,
you leaned over
to tell me instead:
merge them,
be less exact,
allow the paint
to run free,
let the brush
tell you where to go.

Applewood, Butterflies and Summer Rain

for Mike Troyanovich, my grandfather

I

Those first light rain-taps on a thin flat tin roof go
                                        pitapat . . . pitapat.
Ploppy-drops, tintinnabulations that make dust dance
before swimming away, warn goats who loathe
the splatter-sound of wetness and bleat to stay dry.

Wind swirls chaff from sweet hay off barn beams, while smoke
drifts scent of burning applewood from the yard.
A small fire, tended for cooking skewers of bacon, is dampened
                                        by drizzle
that sends a gray-whiskered grandfather and young boy to run
from rain and shelter in the barn. A butterfly tags along.

II

In a sudden summer shower, a yellow swallowtail
paddles the current of air to an open door, asks to share dryness.
He lights on the back of my hand.

Shhh . . . Shhh—rainwater gushes from the downspout.
                        Summer whispers something out of sync.
Shhh . . . Shhh—someone is here.

The swallowtail pulses his wings slowly on the back of my hand
                                        to match heartbeats.

This soft joining of rhythms charms two lives: one from today,
one from before, and lifts a promise like a butterfly in smoke.
A memory rises above the talking sheets of falling water
as two people glisten: together again in summer rain.

    I think: *how is it possible to be with someone who is gone?*
    But the butterfly and I persevere easily
    until sunlight becomes serious again.
                            Wings dry to dust on my fingers.

I see the breadknife in the old man's hand cut a slice of rye
                              from a fresh-baked loaf.
I taste bacon dripping on rye—salt in the rain—

sating a wistful hunger.

Rolling on Red Dog

They toiled with picks and shovels in the darkness of Willow Grove, cutters digging coal from under the mountain. In obscurity with mine timbers, railroad cars and conveyor belts, boys became men, and men grew old underground. They separated shale rock from bituminous coal, created tipplesful of black lumps loaded into railroad cars, leaving slag heaps of shale and coal dust that ignited and burned spontaneously for decades, smoldered into red dog gravel.

Carbide lights fixed to hardhats, metal lunch pails with names etched into lids swinging from hands covered with coal dust, miners broke out of tunnels at day's end, destined home to women barefoot on wooden floors of company row houses. They toiled together, lived the hard life, were paid in scrip to be redeemed only at the company store, enslaving them.

Money taken from miners' pay to cover funerals when they died kept their wives from suffering the cost. The coal companies didn't waste a thing, except maybe a human life or two, here and there, even spreading their red dog gravel on country roads to keep down mud and dust. They liked a clean operation.

When the explosion and cave-in occurred from bad air venting and buildup of methane at Willow Grove Mine in Southeastern Ohio's Belmont County, the coal companies brought out seventy-two caskets, filled the churches for the barefoot women. The hearses rolled on dustless red dog-covered roads up into the hills, closer to the sky—the airflow there spectacular—names etched on stones paid for in advance.

Sacrifice

I lived in this cage, breathed
the air of Willow Grove.

I sat on my perch, sang and preened.
Like Persephone, I awaited

my carriage underground
to the silence and sway of darkness.

Swooning in the noxious air
of the tunnel, I planted myself deeper

into the other world as I searched
for those who preceded me.

When at last the door to my cage
was opened, I flew from my perch,

threw my voice to sing
from the other side.

As I watched myself flutter
downward to the bottom

in faint canary air,
a voice from over there

sang back to me, saying I was free
to go now, find my own way out.

Memoir of a Coal Child

Born out of coal
in the Appalachian foothills,
unadorned, I warmed
by fires that spewed
black soot on white snow,
while leaking from chimneys
a rotten smell
that smothered a land always
in the mood of gray winter.
I left, unable to fit my shape
into the contour of a town
with forty row houses
each with dead flowers
on the porch,
three beer joints,
one co-op store,
no church, and
a two-room schoolhouse
on a mined-out hill.

Through years of toiling
away from this,
I kept my promise.
My flower bloomed
from the house
with no running water
and hand-dug
earthen basement,

placed itself
on the doorstep
of a far world away
that opened up its bounty.

Our Genetic Tag

I run my hand along the strand of wire at the boundary of land I live on now. I count the leaning fenceposts connected by coldness stretching back to where I came from, far behind the hill—the Applegarth farm on the copper creek with a sycamore tree as big as the house. I walk into the hollow tree to find roots as large as railroad ties growing into the creek, tentacles wrapped around discarded, broken farm implements, unable to be let go. The wire from the final fencepost is nailed to the tree, connecting it to a line of posts coming down the hill along the rutted road. The posts stand in fog like mourners as Great Grandfather Dinger Applegarth's casket levitates in pallbearers' hands into the living room of the house to rest a while. When the family passes by to kiss the cold forehead of their father, grandfather, they are unaware that in the skin meeting their lips is a DNA aberrancy. The doctor tells them he died of cancer of the blood, the chromosomal marker called Philadelphia Chromosome connected to myeloid leukemia not discovered until years later when others in the family would die from the same malady.

After burial, children return to the sycamore by the creek to swim with its far-reaching roots as they branch into current, joining the tree to the muddy bank on the other side. A few run along the fence, playing tag around the connecting posts, while I hold hands with my father and grandmother. As we walk the hill back along the double strand of wire toward home, neighbor children lament: *sorry for your loss,* then touch the three of us with their vague little hands, calling out: *you're it!*

Still in Dim Light

They came for him in dim light at daybreak, his hair dripping wet, cream falling from his half-shaven face. From the window upstairs where I'd slept, I could see two vehicles pull into the driveway: a sheriff's car and an all-black sedan, government-looking. Four men came to take my grandfather from our farmhouse in light so pale, dreamlike, I could barely see them. Two, in gray uniforms with wide hats and silver badges, had him by the arms. Grandpap was barefoot, shirtless and handcuffed. The other two men wore long, dark coats, held sledgehammers that found their way to our earthen fruit cellar beneath the house.

I heard and felt metal twisting as they tore copper pipes, threw them from a ground-level window into the yard below me, smashed my grandmother's heirloom asters that lined the drive where the rude cars were parked. Long coats carried clear bottles of liquid, distillates from the copper and cooking corn, placed them in the back of the slick black sedan. As they drove the old man away, no words, no fanfare. Then, in the absence of thunder, a flash of lightning from an approaching storm streaked the sky, illuminating the purple asters and copper pipe strewn in the yard below my narrow window. In that moment of bright light, I could see cars slowly driving down the lane—away. In no hurry—they left me with a lifetime to think about what they had to do.

The Sky Was Always Underground

Nic skryte sa nikdy nestrati.
(Nothing hidden is ever lost).
—Luke 8:17

for my grandfather, Mike Troyanovich

Even my fingers are shaped like yours, they say. I grip
      the shovel
in the afterdamp that becomes more and more faint. I dig
      deeper into the mine tunnel—
still there is no light, no secret passage to air. For you
      the sky was always underground,

your breath laced with communion wine. One Sunday
      morning during Easter season, we stood
in front of Saint Nicholas Russian Orthodox Church
      in the Ohio coal town of Barton.
We had just confessed all our sins, received
      Holy Communion.
You hadn't drunk a drop in a year until the chalice
      of Father Kossi touched your lips
with communion wine. Your voice sounded unrepentant
      to your wife
when you announced in broken English: *Janka, peek me up*
      Duesday, ten 'clock nighttime, right cheer!

Then you walked into the neon lights of the hard-liners
	to begin your three-day binge.
You laid your paycheck on the bar, bought a round
	for the house
as if you'd never been away. An embittered somebody
	in our car
mumbled a choked-up whisper in Slovak: *nic skryte sa
	nikdy nestrati*
as we began the drive home, one person short, not dreaming
	that one day
it would all be written down, yet never assimilated.

As we rolled out of the church parking lot, grandchildren
    stared out the windows
at the fedora riding atop your swagger. My somebody
    grandmother squeezed her hands
more tightly around the steel-cold, crescendoed tremor
    of a lifetime of disdain.
We could feel her exhale the stale air from her lungs,
    listen to it cross the vibrating cords of her larynx,
stumble over her quivering lips. After she held her breath
    to steady herself,
she ejected the sour air of that under-her-breath utterance
    into our ears like an empty shell casing
from a pistol cartridge striking the cold floor, its bullet fired
    point blank into your swagger as:
you son of a bitch in English, plain as day.

The Ditch

The revolving door at Piatek's bar in Fairpoint, Ohio, swung open. Mike Troyanovich tripped into the unsteadiness of the cool night air in May of 1951. On another three-day binge, he'd blown his miner's paycheck and lost the coal rights to his farm in a poker game. As he stumbled up the road toward home, he fell, rolled into a ditch where he spent the remainder of the night that never ended.

He felt safe in ditches. He'd hid in them with friends, a group of young Slovaks and Ukrainian Jews fleeing from the Russian soldiers in 1911. They slept in ditches by day, traveled by moonlight through the grain fields of Ukraine to the Black Sea and a great ship that transported them past the Statue of Liberty in America.

Mike had married one of the young women from the ditch, Vera Fallat of Lucina, a few years after they arrived in New York. She cooked for the wealthy. He became a dock worker, later a carpenter. After marrying, they moved to the copper mines of Montana, then to coalfields in Southern Ohio, the outskirts of a little town called Midway. Together they bought a small farm, a Jersey milk cow, chickens, and tilled a garden to grow food for winter. A daughter, my mother, had been born a year earlier in a chicken house on his brother Steve's land. Now, they had a farm of their own at the edge of Midway. It was their dream, their home from the old country moved to America. From the ditch, in the aftermath of his binge, Mike could see it all so clearly. After losing the coal rights, he wanted to stay in the ditch forever.

Before long the big shovel, bulldozer and haul trucks found their way to the farm, tore away the top coal, that easy-to-mine surface mineral. The process poisoned the well. Vera had to walk a half mile to a springhouse each day to carry back drinking water in buckets. She also lost her grazing land, was forced to pasture her milk cow tied to a long chain on the spoil banks of adjacent deserted coal-company property.

She cursed my grandfather until the day he died, and even after, for losing the coal rights, stripping their farm in the foothills of Appalachia. My grandfather foresaw all this from the ditch that night: his new world, one of port wine and Carling Black Label Beer. Years later when he died, they merely covered him up. Even then, from the ditch, he could hear the sound of heavy machinery, the loud discussions about the top coal, and the weeping that never stopped.

Garden Hoe

I saw the sharp tip of a garden hoe
rise above the top of tall grass.

I heard cursing in Slovak,
first from the old woman with the hoe

chasing the blacksnake through the garden
off her land, then

from her husband, the old man on the porch
screaming to let the snake live,

to please let it live, it would eat the rats
that raided the corncrib in the barn.

Our Father, who art in heaven
    hallowed be thy name

But no: the old woman was determined,
determined to get the snake off her land

the same way she ran off other trespassers
with her hoe, the ones

as we forgive those
who trespass against us

who dared take a shortcut across her land
on their way to the rest of the world

that didn't matter. This was her piece
of ground, hers alone, the property

she owned, paid taxes on, had the deed to,
unlike her family from the old country, Slovakia,

where her people were serfs, potato diggers
for the land barons. Today her hoe had a cause,

a farm to fight for, a weightier purpose
for a hoe, one only dreamt about before.

for thine is the kingdom, and the power,
   and the glory, forever—

Springhouse

A shady wooded spot down the way from wild strawberries—
a diminutive house of weathered boards and sandstone,
            A-framed roof and hinged door.

Vera's sacred spring—
            home to a small striped snake,
stretched along the cool flat of stone where a frog might sit
to watch a spotted salamander crawl to the bottom
            of this diamond-clear pool.
Sometimes, we keep a glass jar of concord grape juice
            there to cool.

            A silken place I love,
like opening the door to a dream of Pirene,
clean and secret in an unassuming ground crevice.
            Our voices lighten to whispers
when we come close, so not to disturb Pegasus drinking.

After filling our shiny smooth buckets, neither of us wants
            to let go our handhold with sanctity.
We share a dipper for the long walk home from our place
            where water springs from an aquifer.
A limestone cloud hides beneath the Appalachian earth
            in a nook so quiet and still
no one dares disrupt the spell of kindness it casts,
            except to drink.

Frank the Dog's Story

Russell, Russell, it's Frank, my grandmother screamed as she ran up the flight of stairs to my grandfather's room. *He's in a fight with the German Shepherd! They're in the ditch!* It was midday. Russell was asleep. He worked the hoot owl shift at Willow Grove Coal Mine. Eyes blinking in disbelief, he calmly turned his head toward the door and asked: *is Frank on the top or the bottom? The bottom,* Elsie replied. *Settle down now, Elsie. He'll be all right. Frank can take care of himself,* he muttered, and went back to sleep. Frank was all right; the shepherd didn't fare so well: while on the bottom, Frank had his adversary on top of him by the throat as he did many of the varmints he'd fought in the past. The neighbor lady across the street on Gobbler's Knob in Fairpoint had bought the shepherd attack dog to keep Frank from engaging in his hobby, chasing her cats and treeing them. Frank, however, became the shepherd's last attack victim. After the encounter he was content to lie on the porch and bark hoarsely at passersby. Here's the thing: this story was told as Russell Graham was lowered into his grave in a cemetery on a ridgetop outside Glencoe, a town in the middle of Southeastern Ohio's coal country. It showed how much Russell had thought of Frank, and just how important a family figure he was.

In his last days, after he and Elsie were divorced, Russell operated a beer joint in Glencoe. He married one of his thirty-year-old bar maids when he was sixty-two. As a result of this unplanned union, three months later I was gifted twin aunts 10 years younger than me. My mother never approved, so whenever Russell came to visit, if my dad wasn't there, she'd push me outside to talk to my grandfather. I'd walk him around our place, show him my Hereford cow, Flemish Giant rabbits, White Rock laying hens and my dad's hunting dogs.

Russell was a dog man, through and through. As we looked over Dad's dogs, he told me about Frank, the brindle Mountain Cur that played a major role in helping the family through the Great Depression. They sold the furs of critters he caught or treed and ate the wild meat he brought home. Russell told me Frank treed a bobcat once, another time a black bear that swam the Ohio River and wandered into the mining country of Belmont County. He said Frank was tougher than any man he ever met, more intelligent than most, and definitely more loyal. He said he loved Frank, and Frank loved him in return.

Russell treated Frank like a brother and often took him to the prize fights on Sunday afternoons after church behind Nicholozakis' bar, down the hill from where he lived. Nicholozakis' place had a mud floor and gaps between the wall boards so wind could blow in, air out the sulfur stink that came from the coal stove. Standing over six feet tall and weighing two hundred pounds like all the other men in his clan, Russell was usually a contestant in the fights. He told me Frank made him a lot of money by coming along because the town folk consulted Frank about who might win the fight. He was that smart: one bark for Russell, two for his opponent.

Frank had charisma. Many people came to the fights to see him, then bet on Russell, giving Russell a greater incentive to win as he would be awarded a percentage of the total purse, usually two thirds. Some Sundays, if the turnout was good and he won, Russell made up to fifty dollars, more than a week's pay in the mine. Frank was his tough little moneymaker, and Russell was about as tough as his dog.

One Sunday, however, the brawling didn't go so well for Russell. His opponent, Tony Pomone, had a real mean streak. His wife had recently thrown him out for coming home drunk one too many times after work. That day Mr. Pomone kicked Mr. Graham's butt all over the side of the mountain of coal behind Nicholozakis' beer joint. They carried Russell home to Elsie on an old army stretcher. Frank ran to the house ahead of his partner to warn Elsie. He jumped into her arms to console her when she saw Russell's eyes swollen shut and lower lip split open, bleeding. Russell missed work for the first time in his life and was in bed for a week.

My father told me this was the time when Frank went downhill himself. He was old, worn down, fought out. One night while Russell was sleeping, he heard a strange, mournful cry coming from the wild hill behind the house—a godawful howl. He didn't know if he was in the middle of a bad dream or if Frank was in the middle of his own bad dog dream about dying. Russell said Frank dreamed of the black dog moon and the coyote sun and went out looking for them, said because it was a dream, Frank never actually died. Russell said he didn't believe what the Iroquois thought about how you died in a dream before you really died. However, no one ever saw Frank again, and Russell, though he was a born dog man, never owned another. He put Jack Daniels on his empty leash and let Jack lead him around, his only friend, until he died. Russell was lowered into the ground that day with Frank's lead strap in his hand. I know. I saw it.

Hell's Kitchen

We drove by Hell's Kitchen on our way to church one Sunday morning. As we gazed at sin from inside the safety of our church clothes, our Ford coupe hummed like a choir in the balcony. Once the boarding house of Mrs. Wormsley, where a drunken coal miner hurled a steel fire poker through the eye and into the brain of his boss, the house was now home only to ghosts of Wheeling, whores nursing beer bottles and miners with liquor on their breath.

As my parents eyed the old house, perhaps looking for someone they knew, my mother blurted that we boys should never go to a place like this, and the only reason she took us now was to show what evil looked like up close.

I found the three-story Victorian house with worn shutters attractive, and as we drove away, looked back to see a white lacey curtain billow out from an open window, flapping like a loose tongue in the morning breeze. The house was airing out, preparing for the next group of miners. They would watch smooth black silk on a slim firm derriere flip her omelette in a pan with a handle long enough to be the offering basket passed down the pew at mass held that Sunday morning at Hell's Kitchen.

Bluebells and Blackdamp

Morning wind pulled the rope on the mountain, rang the starting bell at Kinsman School. The bell breathed out soot-tarnished chimes at recesses as well as announcing the beginning and end to days. Those days were filled with phonetic charts, fraction-covered chalk boards, potbellied stoves, and a large wooden paddle displayed on a desk elevated on a throne in front of the room. The bell, too, signaled the beginning and end to recitations of Longfellow, Thoreau and Keats. For some the end was permanent; for others their poetry would be reignited in other places, in their lives or work.

Gathering pencils from wooden desktops carved with initials of our parents and grandparents, at Kinsman School we were taught by Ms. Warnock, just as they had been taught, to strive for perfection in every aspect of our lives, to judge our own handwriting on the chalkboard, to walk single-file in and out of the two-room school that housed all eight grades. Our strict education prepared us for the sadness of the poetry of working in the mines and the regimentation of digging coal in Southeastern Ohio. After school we tumbled down the mountain, swung from grape vines, clutched shagbarks to keep from falling off our steep world as we scurried toward the company row houses in the valley below.

Dug into the earth at the base of the mountain was a large hole, an abandoned mine shaft where the blackdamp devil lived. Our mothers warned us repeatedly to stay away; the air there, they said, would suck the oxygen out of a child's lungs, turn him blue. They told us the deceivingly beautiful bluebells that lined the train tracks exiting the vile hole were actually the tiny lungs of children who dared to venture too close to the abandoned mine the Hanna Coal Company had not bothered to board shut.

This warning was an irresistible invitation for the town's red-headed daredevil, Stosh the speedster, to run into the hole, disappear for a long minute, then race out to hurl himself into the bed of bluebells lining the tracks, having held his breath so long his lips and face turned an even darker shade of blue than the flowers. The first time, we thought he'd been transformed into a bluebell, but instead were rewarded with that big, stupid grin as he cheated death, lying in the bluebells in front of us, laughing into the face of the blackdamp devil. Our wild risk-taker flew into the tunnel, his quick feet stomped on the feet of the devil while his screams echoed off the mine's timbers for effect. He had kicked the myth of the mountain in the shins. He roared like a black bear coming out of a den in spring, his roar announcing to the world he was king, that he could run from death in the coal and crinkle the worried faces of our mothers.

We Saw the Secret Swimming Hole

School was out. Days were sticky-clothes hot, prompting a plucky itch to swim. Several of us, boys and girls, were war babies, boomers-to-be. We craved adventure. In those times we had no swimming pool or bathing suits, so we swam in the strip-mine ponds and creeks around town. We went almost every summer day, swimming in the buff. The girls swam too but in different places. We just weren't sure where. If we followed them, they would engage in a sit-down strike, not move for hours until we let them be.

Having only brothers, my interest in the town girls was especially keen, forever trying to decipher what they were made of, inside and out. I wasn't alone in my quest as most of the other twelve-year-old boys from my town felt the same way, sisters or no, the opposite sex always the topic of discussion—so aloof, enigmatic. An even greater befuddlement were the scantily clothed girls of summer.

We challenged our town's daredevil, Stosh, to ferret out their swimming hole. He realized immediately what a successful find would do for his reputation. One sultry July afternoon, he eyed their departure, patiently gave them a considerable lead as he sipped his RC Cola. When the time felt right, he looked into the sun, snorted like a billy goat, then bounded into the hills with the stride of an antelope. After following the girls to their secret destination, Stosh hustled back, proudly returning to lead us to their honey-scented swimming hole. At last, we were able to spy on them: found some walking about, melonlike, and others lying in the smooth-skinned sunlight. One dripped water from her bare elbows and earlobes onto lilies as she waded in the shallows of the secluded pond.

Promised that we'd be able to watch undetected from our hiding place in the willows, we turned to thank our scout for a job well done, but he was gone, vanished. We couldn't believe he would desert after

he escorted us to the movies, ordered the popcorn and hosted the fea-
tured show. Suddenly we heard Stosh shriek: *eeeeeeeeeeeeeeeeek,* as he
leapt into the pond from the top of the high wall, his naked white butt
streaking into the sanctuary. His screech was followed by many more
from the girls, then squawks and squeals as they gathered their clothes,
giggling into the hills, their voices disappearing and reappearing: *go
awaYYYYY . . . GO awayyyyyy,* in and out as they rounded the wild-
curved corners, traversed the narrow straightaway valleys. The hills had
dissolved them, made them their own to remember.

Walnut in Ice

A nearby church bell chimed evening vespers as a walnut fell far out into Wheeling Creek, fell just short of fast-moving current, fell from an ancient tree with three trunks. The ground below the tree lay open, as if waiting for the placement of a cross below the one trunk that was curved and leaned out over the creek in the shape of a nun bowing her head to God. The tree, the nun, watched the walnut fall as the church bell rang, the tree rooting toward the current, drawn to it. The creek, painted orange from sulfur leaching from mines, caressed the walnut in its bubbling froth, locked it inside an eddy.

Winter came—cold, snowy—and embedded the walnut in ice, suspended half in, half out of water, undecided. The creek froze over except for the very center, where deep current ran too swift for ice to form. Children skated on the iced-over creek after school, raced to the next coal town where a fire awaited under a cement bridge, *Jesus Saves* graffitied on its cold girder. Hot chocolate poured from a thermos; homemade bread shared; tingling feet warmed by fire.

Then they skated three miles home, always a race. The fastest skater, a showman, liked to jump the six-foot-wide unfrozen center of the creek, landing on the other side many times over. Like a drum major leading a band, he displayed himself well in front of the other children, skimmed the ice with long and graceful strides.

As they lagged behind, the children watched him lean into the bank, prepare a half spin to jump the stretch of open current. He snapped a pirouette, shifted his weight like an Olympian. When the tip of his skate struck the walnut, hidden by a dusting of snow as thin as a cloak of incense, the showman stumbled forward, crashed and hit the ice, slid head first into the fast-moving current.

He went down, trapped under ice. Calmed by water's cold hypnosis, he was baptized in the deep orange. There were no cell phones, paramedics or even ambulances to summon. No 911 to call. Only screaming children, ladders, an inner tube from the back of a nearby garage, and the funeral director's wagon.

The showman surfaced three days later not far from where the skaters gathered at the old cement bridge. In a swirling eddy near a wide channel of deep open current, his blue face was lodged against the far abutment of the bridge, his arms spread, embracing it. A prayer was said for him in church on Sunday—*Hospodi Pomilui (Lord Have Mercy)*—and a cement cross placed in the open space which had been waiting at the foot of the walnut tree that grew beside the creek where he had disappeared under ice.

Now, in the evenings, at vespers, as the church bell rings, wispy clouds like long musical skating strides are sometimes seen in winter, as if someone is skating where earth meets the heavens, where the creek runs orange into an orange sky, where the bowing nun sings, holds a crucifix carved from walnut as her feet dangle in the numbing swiftness of current.

Blue Racer

A cold-blooded spy, he lay at the very back of my head as I slept on the cool and shady side of a creek bank one warm spring day. Done with the stolen afternoon of fishing, I'd found a grassy niche below the gravel road. Awakened by the strange feeling that someone was watching me, I turned my head to see him, a blue hoop of muscle, bone and scales coiled around a serpentine head, lidless slits for eyes that never blinked now fixed on mine. As he watched from the ledge inches above me, I wondered if I had come to his place, or he mine.

As I contemplated my next move, he uncoiled to writhe down the steep bank, glissaded on a cushion of air onto water, with his front portion oddly sticking up like a bent blue pump handle with eyes protruding from its end. Nature had equipped him with his own built-in periscope, his head swiveling side to side.

I imagined he was looking for more grade school boys like me. His five-foot length and heavy thickness caused me to shake all over: surely he was the truant officer of the devil and would make me pay for this one time in my life I played hooky from Wheeling Township School to fish. Guilt turned to fear as I gathered my pole, lifted a stringer of fish from the water and scurried away, feeling like my face and body had turned blue, marking me like the racer as I slithered through tall grass toward home, my head sticking up like a periscope in a nightmare.

Though I know memory has no form, even with the passage of time, the blue racer has managed to crawl back into my dream world. More than once I've been awakened from sleep by the feeling some thing or some body is watching me. Red tongue flickering like a laser of light, I'll find him coiled there, on the ledge of the nightstand, with those blue lidless eyes fixed on the back of my head. As I awaken to defend myself, I turn to watch him slither away.

Face Down in the Haymow

In the Ohio June sun, tar bubbled on the roof of the barn: *bup . . . bup . . . bupbupbup.* Inside, in the haymow, a bale careened off the elevator, hit the boy stacker in the forehead, frazzled him. A tear wobbled in his eye but wouldn't fall. The next bale struck his chest—*ooooooofffffff*—knocked him off his feet. Coated in sweat and chaff, the boy fell face down in the hay. Heavy bales collided, overturned like boxcars off train tracks—smashing into each other until they covered him. He moaned from the top of the barn: *moooooaaaah, moooooaaaah*—like a sick calf. No one heard him.

First day on the job for the ten-year-old. Not realizing he'd collapsed, the farmers came to his rescue only after bales jammed the elevator leading up to the loft, high in the banked barn. The boy stacker, no longer stacking them, instead, was down under bales at the top of the mow, unconscious.

Nose bleeding, face pale as a newborn Hereford calf, the farmers pulled him out. *Is he dead? Looks like it. No, he's not! He's breathing!* They dragged him outside to the well with the long green pump handle under the spreading oak—limbs, arms coming down from the sky. The boy could blearily see daylight filtering through tree branches onto the rusted pump handle working up and down like a mechanical heart—up and down, up and down—*orrrrinnnnk, orrrrinnnnk, orrrrinnnnk*—pulsing water, deep from the well, cool onto his face and chest. The farmers shook him, ripped off his clothes. He lay buck naked, gazed upward into limbs of the oak—began to believe they were the arms that would save him.

Then his name, faintly at first, from the far side of the mountain—the past, sensing danger, calling from his mother's porch: *Jonny, Jonny! Hold on, Jonny!* Again, the tear wobbled in his eye but wouldn't fall. The voice came closer. He heard it above the din of the tractor, the rackety rhythm of the hay elevator, as if, now, the future were crying out from his father's pickup: *get up, get up Jonny! You have a life to live!* The farmers shook him a second time. The boy awoke. Washed out, confused, he spent the remainder of the day propped on a haybale in the shade of the oak, sipped water from the well, watched the hay wagons come and go from fields down by the train tracks.

Gradually his body and mind came back. The bruises of his flesh moved inward. He healed everywhere at once—hardened. The following week he returned to work. Kept out of the mow, he became permanent stacker on the wagon behind the baler, out in the moving air of open fields where he could breathe, run to a nearby pond for a quick dip on a wide turn, and in years to come grow to lift a bale in each hand—and think about how the haymow wobbled a tear that was death in his eye.

A Roar from the Hill

Like hummingbirds checking trumpet flowers for nectar, our feet felt each corn husk cut down to the soil by the corn picker. Though most were hollow, we sought the ones fat with yellow kernels, the ones we could rip from stalks and slip into burlap bags. She and I would walk the rows together as Baba and Janka, hoping the imposing red picker would miss an entire row of cobs as it swung itself carelessly, or was it purposely wide, as it negotiated a turn on wheels cheeping and chirping in the Appalachian air that dripped our sweat.

She and I, like two hummingbirds, gleaned the fields together, singing. We dragged the bursting burlap bags to the very edge of a hard day's labor to be hauled, stacked in her corn crib in bins lined with sheets of tin to keep the rats away. She wore her red babushka. I dressed in a blue shirt she fashioned for me from a feed sack the color of her eyes, threads holding it together, tough and weary like the dirt-filled lines on our hands.

We walked the bent-down rows of corn, teetering and balancing like a circus act. We imagined townspeople squinting down at us from their perches on the hill above us filled with ironweed and thistle, overlooking the field of stubble where we stood. They were a gallery of weeds, entertained by our antics, clapping and laughing as the wind jiggled their stems, amazed that we could be so poor. Until at last, we'd lift from the field, she and I, all nectar extracted from that particular bloom of ground, whirring, darting away to the next flower, the next field, putting on quite the show for our audience of weeds, the crowd above us that roared in both awe and disbelief.

Moonwalker and the Sleeping Bees

Down the long lane, on past fields of wild sunflowers and roadside morning glories, the bees sleep at night. Walking into evening, a summer breeze in my face, I could sense sweetness from afar. As a young boy, my father sent me on my first mission alone to Old Sam's apiary to bring home a jar of the finest locust-blossom honey in all the land, honey poured directly from the faucet of the bees into a mason jar with a wax comb that couldn't wait to be pressed by a pewter spoon. My brothers and I were fascinated by watching the thick honey ooze onto our father's plate, its royal viscosity dark and fit for a king or a priest.

As I came upon the bee-man's home, I saw it was a white square box not unlike his hives but with a weathervane on the roof as pointed as the steeple on a church. In luck, I found him amongst his parishioners, the bees, in a ceremonial suit that made him look like our first moonwalker, Neil Armstrong, as he took those stiff-legged steps on the moon's surface after exiting Apollo 11. The astronaut wore a bulky helmet and spacesuit to protect him from the perilous environment in space, his face in the helmet the same as the bee-man's and nearly as round as the moon.

For his safety in the apiary, the bee-man held a bellows smoker, gently squeezing anesthetizing smoke, bee incense, into an opened hive, lifting out the honey-laden frames to carry to his extractor. To me, this ritual made him seem like a priest at communion. As the bees followed him with their compound eyes, he slowly moved back and forth, swinging his smoker like a thurible, lulling the honey makers into a trance. Smoke calmed the bees, and as I watched their mesmerized weaving about, I felt as though I had fallen under a spell myself.

Slipping away like a bee in smoke, I savored sweet sustenance in my mouth, a square of fresh honeycomb offered to me by the bee man to energize my long walk home. Drifting back, I looked up to the sky like a bee, to see the round face of a lonely man in the moon. Was he Neil Armstrong? Regardless, I felt I was walking beside him, on the moon, as I carried the locust-blossom honey from the keeper to my father in the night air of the sleeping bees.

Grain Farmer

John Korns was a large man, built more like Jupiter than a farmer. He started out small like most of us, but over the years bought farms around his that went belly up when times were hard and land was cheap. He acquired thousands of acres, became big.

Quiet, common, John wore baggy, blue bib overalls—his signature dress. He tilled the soil, planted corn and soybeans, worked side by side with his grown daughter, driving the planters, harvesters and big tractors together.

One day, at harvest time, John Korns disappeared. His daughter called for him: no answer. She sped to the grain bin where he'd been hauling harvested corn. There sat his empty truck with no sign of her father. She assumed the worst. It wouldn't be like John Korns to leave his work.

After sucking out all the grain, they found him at the bottom of the bin, beneath tons of shelled corn with a blue pant leg from his bib overalls caught in a steel circulator arm.

The coroner said he died of suffocation. To me, he seemed too large to go like that, like he always had more than enough air in his lungs to last a normal lifetime.

It didn't seem possible or right to any of us that John Korns would die in his own grain, a substance of nourishment. I thought he would go in one of the more usual ways. Instead, he went the way some farmers would prefer.

In Roman mythology, Ceres is the goddess of the harvest, of grain, of corn. She is a star in the night sky. As a tiller of land, John Korns was a heavenly body in her constellation. When he fell, the circulator arm in the grain bin became the corn knife that cut him from his stalk, releasing his spirit as a bright star to fill the dark space he left in the Ceresian night sky with new light.

He Followed the Tracks

The odors of sweat, creosote and cow dung hung in the air around him, accompanied him from the railroad tracks and barns where he slept. If conditions were right, you could sense his coming long before he arrived, like smelling wet dog even before the dog was wet. Or—you could listen for him, hear his antics from far off in the darkness as he danced and howled in Slovak to the music he heard in his mind: *ahehhhh . . . ayeeeee . . . oleeeee . . . Slovaci!*

Unhoused, lean and tall with matted, dendritic hair the color of a sardine can turned inside out, a brain like a bag of loose tools looking for a screw to turn, a spike to drive, Pete the Drifter followed the tracks from town to town and back again. Even in summer he wore a long gray coat in harried wind. The dirt of delusion painted his face. A pronged wedge of hair frantically bore down from the top of his head to a point that lengthened his beaklike nose, gave him the expression of birdlike craziness.

He stopped here and there for an odd job, a cup of warm brew and piece of lonesome pie on some widow's sun-starved porch in return. Always back to the tracks to build an astrocytic fire, sleep in the convoluted linens of his mind, he would ask and answer his own questions aloud. Showered by sounds of passing locomotives: *whooooooooooommmmmmmmppphhh,* their vibrations riveted the jumbled words trapped in the circuitry of his brain to the ties that held the tracks to the earth. He would follow them out. They led him away from the delirium that pinned him inside himself.

The tracks were his institution, his therapy as he walked from town to town. Steady. Never better. Never worse. Never a bother, or a burden. He looked back at the world as it looked at him, in neuropsychiatric wonderment. Always following the tracks, Pete the Drifter prayed they would lead him home.

When the train of lost souls and born-agains, the train that chased time's shadow, the one he had been waiting for all the years finally came, Pete the Drifter stepped from the tracks onto a boxcar, traded his murky, troubled world for a more pure and perfect darkness. Then the train made a sound—not in any language—but a sound that life makes for those who listen: *whoooooooooooommmmmmppphhh!* Pete the Drifter rode this train as far as it would go, never expecting to ride it back.

Alex the Swede

One Memorial Day, as I trudged a weedy path in the cemetery toward my family's markers, I heard a groan, like someone with their leg pinned beneath a collapsed mine timber. I heard it again, then watched the tree near Alex's stone move and groan with the wind. As I walked closer, a hint of lavender wafting through the air, I stopped to remember his story. Alex felt like family.

My first job had come when I was six years old emptying the chamber pot and coal-stove ashes for Alex the Swede. Alex rented a room attached to the neighbor's dirt-floor pole garage where my father leased a space for his racing-green '53 Ford coupe. He had no garage, and Dad said he didn't want the sparrows unloading their blackberry preserves on his car. He loved that Ford. He also loved Alex the Swede, as did I.

Alex (the Swede) Svensson was a coal miner like everyone else in town. He worked at the Troll Town mine near a small village of row houses that carried the same name. Born there, my dad explained to me that trolls were dwarfs who sang to the miners as they worked underground. On the last shift Alex worked, when the trolls stopped singing, a cave-in occurred. Trapped between the coal car he was loading and a heavy support timber that fell from the roof of the mine shaft, he screamed, then groaned: *my leg! My leg!* Crushed, mangled, he wouldn't let the surgeon take it off until it festered. After Alex the Swede lost his leg, he'd drag his new wooden leg down to the beer joint every day, play poker and swill whiskey, paid for by his coal company pension.

On crutches, hobbling to the beer joint to comfort his leg with liquor, he flagged me one afternoon as I rode my bicycle after first-grade classes ended at Kinsman School. Alex said he would pay fifty cents a day for me to assist him. I didn't know why he chose me as there were plenty of other children available. Perhaps it was because I was so young, and Alex felt certain I would be around until the end of his days.

Alex directed me to come to his room every morning without fail—no excuses. His offer of fifty cents was generous, pretty good money for a six-year-old in 1953. Starting the next morning, I arrived at his room at daybreak, emptied and rinsed his piss pot, raked the ashes out of the bottom of the coal stove, restarted the fire, and refilled the empty buckets sitting beside the stove from the coal pile at the side of the road in front of his room. After bringing in a fresh bucket of drinking water from the well, I swept the floor and took a fifty-cent piece off the table. One was placed there every day, usually next to a half-empty whiskey bottle and stack of books, all in Swedish. Alex left me the fifty-cent piece religiously until I was ten. One morning I went to empty his piss pot and found it unused. Alex wasn't asleep in his bed snoring as he usually was, his wooden leg gone from its propped-up position against the chair.

Alex simply disappeared, not saying a word to anyone. He didn't leave so much as a farewell note or drop a hint that he was going. Ben Slick, who ran the beer joint, said he probably took a sabbatical, went back to Stockholm to study the brannvin, schnapps and lagers there. Alex the Swede was never heard from again.

Years later, hunters walked up on a human skeleton partially covered with leaves in the woods about two miles from town, down in a deep ravine. The skeleton was missing a leg. Everyone thought for certain it was Alex the Swede, but the skeleton had its left leg missing. Alex lost his right leg in the mine accident. Mayor Ben Slick said he was confused by it all, that Alex was often confused himself, even when sober. Ben speculated that maybe he tripped and rolled down the mountain. In doing so his legs became entangled, got wrapped around each other, confused, and made the switch themselves unknowingly. It seemed like sound hillbilly logic to me at the time.

The case never went to court. Most folks living in the hills were poor and foreigners. The justice system wasn't concerned about finding a skeleton unless, in some way, the discovery involved city people. Not long after the bones were found, I received an airmail letter postmarked in Stockholm. It had no return address. When I opened the envelope, the only thing written was *thank you*, a US currency fifty-cent piece taped to the paper. The delicate handwriting appeared to be that of a woman, and the paper held the barely-noticeable scent of lavender.

To this day it's not known what really happened to the old Swede. Did he die? Did he go back to Sweden to family, a woman perhaps? Whose skeletal remains did the hunters find? I can't stop thinking about the way Alex used to sing—so beautifully in his native tongue. One time I asked him what it meant. He said his dialect was Jantlandic, and the song about eternal love. Tears came to his eyes, and he changed the topic of conversation. So little was known about Alex the Swede, why he came to coal country in the first place, and why he never spoke of family.

A runestone was placed on the grave of the remains of the skeleton, assuming it was the Swede. It read: Alexius Svensson? Disappeared September 11, 1957. When I think of him, I recall the ratchety sound my father's car made when it was being started in the ground-cold garage beside Alex's room, the way the exhaust smoke fumed the air like lingering fog. I also remember this: one day, as I picked up my fifty-cent piece, I opened the cover of a novel on the table next to an empty bottle of whiskey. *Utvandrarna*/The Emigrants by Vilhelm Moberg, in Swedish. Inside the cover, handwritten words, similar to the handwriting on the airmail letter: *jag alskar dig*/I love you, *vanlagen komma hem*/please come home—*Elin*. I always associated Alex the Swede with the odor of coal and urine, and the clack of his cane on pavement. When I visit his grave the only scent in the air is a faint sweetness of lavender. The only sound—the groaning of trees.

Country Store and a Wild Rose

A soft and wild yellow rose grew from stone on the porch of our country store, its stem climbing green the awning. The store was good to all of us. In lean times, we leaned in for a loaf of bread, a carton of milk. In happy times, we laughed under the awning, waited for the school bus in spring rain hissing on stone as we stood chewing pink-penny gum and trading baseball cards.

On the porch's long, storied bench, tales were ground into wood, gossip circulated, babies conceived from sparks between sets of eyes connecting on warm nights in sweet light, unintended ambience of a Stroh's Beer lamp shining on a shelf inside the store.

No cash or scrip was needed, only the words: *put it on the bill!* No company store, this co-op stood for progress, manumission from the mining company. A chance for a life. Like the store, the wild rose sprang from rock to climb the wall, arms reaching to the top to bloom in the sun, it too clinging to stone.

Inevitable Rose

When snow fell over the windblown field, it was no one's fault, really,
    but an inevitable rose emerged.
Into this frozen loneliness of winter, this silk of moon, the cold flower
    began to sing
on cue with the wind's bow touching a branch of tree shaped
    like a father's violin.

Together, they performed the song "Ave Maria," a haunting rendition
    once delighting all of us,
when years ago, music cascaded from the balcony of a church
    at a family wedding.

Today, from another life gathering's solemn perspective,
    our recollection strains
to hear the duo deliver the melody again, but then, as if someone
    has forgotten to hold onto the violin,
it falls with its song from the balcony through the icy moonlit octaves
    into the snow's austere arrangement, the flower left to sing alone.

I wonder how the voice of a cold rose could sound so beautiful
    without the violin.
Would she now become imprisoned by the song to never sing again,
    or would she hear "Ave Maria"
over and over in her mind, sing only it forever—

for no one in particular, really, but herself and the ones in the family
    left standing over a small urn
with the configuration of a music box made from violinlike wood
    resting on the pure white snow of tablecloth,

the inevitable rose imprisoned in a delicate vase placed beside the urn,
    waiting for the cue to sing,
waiting for an untroubled wind to unwind this frozen moment
    and scatter us all.

Winter Gift From Fall Woods

Our forked sticks poked new-fallen leaves, windblown around rotting logs and tree trunks, uncovering brown shitake wonders in black loam, earth-scented treasures of the russeting fall woods. A family affair where each October we drove down a secluded logging road to the edge of Uncle Guy Dunn's oak and hickory grove, and parked by the remnant sawmill under a butternut tree.

My brothers and I, each given a woven peck basket to carry mushrooms, foraged the woods like piglets rooting for turnips. Mother and Father sang sweet lines from "The Old Rugged Cross" and "You Are My Sunshine" as we passed Wheeling Valley Cemetery from the Revolutionary War era, stopping to check dates from the late 1700s inscribed in stone. Those markers, smoothed by wind and rain, spurred our imaginations to storm through the woods as we made up stories about the Seneca Indian scout's V-shaped white stone, polished by time like a piece of flint, an arrowhead aimed at the sky.

My grandmother, years of mushroom-picking wisdom tucked under her red babushka, was there with us in her feed-sack dress, its frayed ends dragging the earth like soft little plows in a sylvan garden. She made the final call of edibility on each fungal nugget, tossed many aside after evaluating their undersides, taking a discerning sniff. Keepers would be dried on her porch, canned in mason jars in a vinegary soup with onions and cut potatoes, then served on Slovak Christmas Eve supper with miniature poppyseed rolls.

Mushrooms gathered made this Russian Orthodox Christmas, celebrated two weeks after the traditional American holiday, a festive gift, as if we'd been granted two gems during the feast-day season. We felt honored, like Christ had been born twice, the first time for all the Christian world, a second for the humble Slovaks living in the coal country hills, who followed the Gregorian calendar in their church, gathering the russet of the fall woods to flavor their soup.

In the Shadow of the Moth

We sat in the shadow of the moth under our kitchen ceiling light,
     together at the big table,
  listening to the radio. It was late.
The Cleveland Indians were playing a twilight double-header on the
     West Coast.
     The time of Vic Wertz, Early Wynn and Rocky Colavito.
Friday. No school on Saturday, so I sat next to the man
     in a sleeveless t-shirt
  at our big table playing solitaire deep into night.

He'd gifted me my own deck of cards, all clean and slick as a new
     spring day,
  so I could be like he used to be when he was ten,
sit at the big table with him as he did with his grandfather. His deck
     was worn,
  some numbers barely discernible,
smudged with grime and soot like faces of coal miners crawling
     out of tunnels,
  but the jacks smiled and the queens
folded their arms over their chests triumphantly.

His left thumb scooted cards three at a time from the top of the deck,
     then his right hand
  turned the cards face up onto the big table
to see if any were playable. I watched him tap nicotine-stained fingers
     of his dominant right hand on the cards,
while his whiskered face surveyed the columns of cards
     already played,
  trying to find places to assimilate the newly turned ones.

As I watched his hands move, they seemed tired, weighted, and
        to know about
    more than solitaire, as if thinking for themselves.
I wondered how they managed to bring him so far, attached to his
        worn-out arms,
    all the way from Lucina
on the Bohemian border in Slovakia to the Black Sea, on past the
        Statue of Liberty.

Now they were here in America at the big table, listening
        to a ballgame
    on the West Coast broadcast on the radio, playing
that indelible radio sound in the night air where smoke
        from his one-after-the-other
    Lucky Strikes circled the big table
up to the moth on the ceiling light, the breeze from the open screen
        door dancing
    with the smoke as he swilled his port.

I wondered if there was something more about the hands than the
        laying down
    of cards,
if the port made the hands remember or forget this, if the shadow of
        the moth
    had anything to do with it,
if being in that shadow had something to do with the way
        I remembered
    the light that night.

The First Soft Peeps of Summer
Beneath White Feathers

In our barn, a grain bin housed a white-feathered hen. She nested in a dark corner, sat on eggs in a hay-filled wooden box, a porcelain bowl of rolled oats before her, next to a shallow tin pan with a flat brown stone—centered—weighting the water that was clean, safe, expectant. All this arranged far back in the dark corner, with eggs that stirred beneath the hen, warm and anxious for twenty-one days that seemed like a hundred to a boy like me.

I tiptoed closer to look—my steps more delicate than breath from a mother who purred softly to a new baby. I did not want to disturb the hatching-out about to happen but couldn't resist the first querying yellow head with eyes peeking out beneath white feathers. I heard summer's first soft peep of life, then another, and another . . . to become a chorus of fuzzy little balls with tiny orange beaks.

As I stood at the barn's threshold on the sandstone foundation, I felt the feathered touch of a hand on my shoulder—Vera's dear hand instructing without speaking that the hen and her chicks would need time together alone. To bond them was nature's way, to imprint each to each, the puffs of fuzzy peeping to the purrs and clucks in the fluff of white feathers.

Sitting in the Same Dark

I depended on my grandmother Vera
    being there, in her kitchen, alone

in the dark, time still left in the day, waiting
    for it to end. I'd rattle the loose, round

door knob, our secret handshake, and hear:
    Janka, that you? I'd answer: *Baba, I can't*

see you. You there? She'd laugh. I'd come in
    to her darkness, her saving of electric left over

from Great Depression days. There'd be
    a little light from the dial of the low-playing,

plug-in radio, Vera's shadow cast on the wall
    behind it, her form as straight-backed

as the chair she sat in, both shadows on the wall
    beside the table, it too, up against the wall.

I'd take my seat in the empty chair on the other
    side of the table and face out, the two of us

sitting together, facing out. *What you doing*
    sitting here in the dark? She'd tell me

she was reading the book she had in her mind,
    the one about the old country. She'd tell me

the story time-after-time about how she left
        at nineteen, hid in ditches of Ukraine with other

young Slovaks and Jews by day, then by night traveled
        to the Black Sea in the same dark she sat in now.

I'd ask: who were you hiding from in the ditches? She'd
        say: *the soldiers*, then turn the pages of her book

with her breath. In the dark, I came
        to understand about the soldiers and ditches.

They became to me what they were to her
        as the night took us in, then let us both go.

II.

The Kid Was Born a Jack-of-All-Trades

A star in a basket of miracles,
coal people came from all over
to gawk at the baby who could talk
at six months of age—
the two-headed calf at the carnival,
this child who couldn't yet
sit up straight or feed himself,
let alone walk. Lying in the crib,
flat on his back, a big head
on a small hunk of flesh wrapped
in a diaper, smiling at his visitors,
he appeared unimpressive to all,
that is, until he spoke. Then it
became clear that the talking
portion of his brain had been
slow cooked in the womb to an
odd perfection. When asked his
name, he spoke it. He could even
spill out short phrases. Once
someone, perhaps an uncle,
pinched his toe, and as the story goes,
this child may have uttered
curse words in Slovak: *smirdas
ako hovno!* God forbid!
Now where did that come from?
Uncanny! Visitors thought
he would surely grow up
to talk too much.

Even his mother said,
with all his talking,
the Kid was destined
to become a jack-of-all-trades,
master of none.

The Rat Speaks to the Kid

Above the damp mud floor of a hand-dug basement, perched on the lid of a washing machine in his cotton diaper, the Kid looked down at a steel tub where coal-blackened clothes soaked. They waited their turn in the churning slosh-monster. All was well until his mother walked up the slatted staircase to attend to dinner cooking on a coal stove in the kitchen above the basement. As if he'd been waiting forever for this one vile opportunity, a large brown rat jumped onto the nearby wooden bench to watch over the Kid while his mother was gone. The rat looked the Kid directly in the eye as he sat on his haunches with his long round tail twitching to wrap itself around the Kid's warm neck while his sharp incisors chewed at the Kid's ears and eyeballs. If he could have, the Kid would have run out right then.

Fifty years later, the rat speaks: "Child in the diaper, I am not to be feared. All these years you've misjudged me. I am here to speak to you about my uncle. Like your own, he was at Willow Grove that day, deep down in the tunnel, his ear-drums blown out by the whoosh of the explosion. Blood dripped from his eyes. Timbers crushed his skull and chest, just as they did your uncles'. My mother's mind, too, caved-in as though she'd been in the mine herself. Your uncles and family are not the only ones afflicted by the Willow Grove Mine Disaster. This is what I was trying to tell you that day I stared at you from the bench, but had no words for it then. Now, touch my hand."

But there is no hand.

The Ride to School

Fever kept the Kid home from school for two days. On the morning of the third day, it broke. The seven- year-old's mother thought he was well enough to walk the mile to Kinsman School, high on a hill overlooking their town. As he walked past the clubhouse liquor establishment, sitting on the porch sipping coffee was self-appointed mayor and retired coal miner, Ben Slick.

Ben Slick: *hey Kid, you feelin' any better?*

Kid: *yes, thanks.*

Ben Slick: *you sure are walkin' slow. You must be weak. Would you like a ride to school in my pickup? I've got to make a trip to St. Clairsville anyway. I could drop you off at Kinsman.*

Kid: *okay. Man, your truck is pretty beat up!*

Ben Slick: *yeah. I drove it to work at the Willow Grove Mine for years. Sometimes your dad and grandpap rode with me. Then the explosion occurred, and I quit, retired early.*

Kid: *where is Willow Grove anyway?*

Ben Slick: *it's just outside St. Clairsville on the road to Belaire. Didn't your dad tell you what happened there?*

Kid: *no.*

Ben Slick: *well, one March morning, just a few years before you were born, there was a big explosion and cave-in. Seventy-two miners died. Five were from our little town of Midway. Two of the men killed, only in their twenties, were Johnny Sclenicka and Cecil Grimes, husbands of your aunts, Marjorie and Clara Graham. Many young children were left fatherless. Some of the wives never got over it, still crying themselves to sleep at night. Your grandfather, Russell, really helped Clara, his younger sister, as she had four children. Your other grandfather, Mike, retired, like me. We'd seen enough. We were lucky to have worked a different shift that day.*

Kid: *how'd it happen?*

Ben Slick: *a buildup of methane gas, firedamp, that ignited, causing a powerful whoosh in the tunnel that blew mine support timbers off the ceilings and doors off hinges. The mines are dangerous, Kid. Stay out if you can, even the old, deserted mines. You know Truman McConnell's six-year-old son died a few years ago from blackdamp when he crawled into an old, boarded-up mine on their farm. By the way, next year they're boarding up Kinsman, your little two-room school. I went there when I was a kid, and so did your dad and mom. You'll be going to Wheeling Township School in Fairpoint where there are some good teachers: Mr. Wilkins, a math and science whiz, and Mr. Reed, who will teach you literature and poetry. I hear Mr. Reed requires his students to recite a poem in front of the class each day. Well, here we are, kid, at your little school on top of the mountain. See you, son. Say hello to old Ms. Warnock for me. Remind her that my knuckles still sting from the ruler when she smacked me for popping off that time years ago.*

Kid: *thanks for the ride, Ben Slick.*

Ben Slick: *don't get used to it, Kid. You need to walk your way up the mountain just like I did.*

Schoolhouse Chalkboard

for Ms. Warnock, country schoolhouse teacher

Softly,   rhythmically,   graceful as a miniature ballerina,
  I moved as   chalky-smooth,   pencil-thin
                  silk through sound,
    an enigmatic blessing   melding   white into black,
magically guiding
    eager hands   connected to   higher matter
across   my flat   belly of slate.
       Leaving   myself
                  as we all
                  must,

                  dust,
but mine   arranged   in crystalline   patterns,
   words and numbers   scratched on the wall,
               handwriting,
cursive   and   printed,   or mathematically   symbolled—
               all knowledge.
You could erase me   clean,   but   what chalk put
              down on me
   would become   indelible,   branding minds of
mining children   at Kinsman School   being taught
          to read
          and write.
Who   could forget   the sound of   dotting
       an "i,"

weaving   a flowing "g"   or spilling   an entire
                    poem on the wall!
Like   smoke in the sky,   I disappear into   the great swirl,
    but   marks   left on me   are
                    embers
in darkness,   astral flowers that   luminesce   night
    after night,   year   after year,   until
               all   my students   are gone.

Search for the Edible Rose

Well into the berry-picking process of a dewy morning in the foothills of Southeastern Ohio, and, in the thick maze of a wild patch of *Rubus Occidentalis*, the edible rose, the Kid rounded a turn in thorny brush. The thicket fed on itself to grow, and smelled like an open jar of Grandma's wild black raspberry jam. In the midst of this berry patch taller than any man, the Kid came upon a path already traveled, smashed down so recently he could smell and taste the fresh crush of green.

There, standing only a few feet away with his back turned towards the Kid was a large manlike form with thick apelike hair. He wore dirty leather boots laced to his knees with steel-gray pants tucked inside them. Like the Kid, this intruder was gathering raspberries in the June-morning fog, although he used a brown woven basket, perhaps borrowed or stolen, instead of an empty coffee can like the Kid. He jerked and shoved nearly as many berries in his mouth as he placed in his basket.

Unusual for the intruder to be there. The Kid was far from home in the badlands, in a spot where only his Czechoslovakian grandmother had gone. She was the pie maker and canning lady. She chained her milk cow on nearby alfalfa fields planted by the coal company to hide the unearthed soil and rock. Except for their tromped paths and his grandmother's primitive pasturing, the area was desolate. Big shovels like the Groundhog, Mountaineer and Silver Spade had long ago dug their pits, extracted all the coal from under the once rolling foothills, and left it un-reclaimed—to rot on itself—a geologic vomit.

The Bigfoot in the berry patch, his hair long even on the backs of his hands, wore a gray shirt with a horizontal line of black numbers between his shoulder blades. He had a musty, old wet-tennis-shoe smell about him. But the Kid had gotten too close by accident, didn't care to ask questions, and before the Bigfoot even realized he was there, the Kid was gone.

The boy looked over his shoulder a hundred times on the trek home. His coffee can full of wild black raspberries jiggled in the morning sun. After blurting out the story to his grandmother, she spoke to him in the broken language he had become so accustomed to: *Janka, a bad man, he escape jail in Moundsville. Dis man, he kill people. You lucky you make it back. Now give me berries. I make you good pie.*

Scrip

A twelve-year-old boy leads his red dog up the gravel road toward home on an afternoon in the fall of 1959. He stops in front of the Midway Clubhouse, once the shack where his mother was born, now a beer joint. On the porch, seated on a chair he borrowed from one of the poker tables inside, sits heavy-whiskered Ben Slick. The Kid stops to talk, turns toward him to find five empty brown beer bottles listening from the floor beside the elderly man in the black ball cap, TWILIGHT LEAGUE embroidered on it in gold letters.

Ben Slick: *what's that long-eared dog's name, Kid?*

Kid: *Scrip.*

Ben Slick: *must be worthless. Scrip went out several years ago, son. What kind of dog is he? He's redder than red dog gravel.*

Kid: *he's a foxhound, and a good one!*

Ben Slick: *I figured he was some kind of varmint chaser or foreigner, just like the folks around here. Where'd your old man get him?*

Kid: *he just wandered in and stayed,* then asked: *say, what was scrip anyway?*

Ben Slick, setting another empty down, his audience looking up to him, answers the Kid as if he'd read his mind: *first off, son, never drink more than two of these beers in a day. You'll stay out of trouble and live longer that way. Scrip was a form of money used around here for years, coal company money. That's what they paid me in when I worked at Willow Grove Mine before I retired. They were paper bills and token coins made from copper and nickel mostly. They were stamped with a company symbol or name and had a number showing how much they were worth. Only place I could use my scrip was at the company store. I had to buy everything there and was no better off than a slave. They charged too much for everything. That's why we formed our own Midway Co-op Store here in town. Your dad is president of the store.*

Then he paused and asked: *say, when will your dad run that hound again?*

Kid: *we're going tonight. It's a full moon and will be easy to find our way in the moonlight.*

Ben Slick: *mind if I come along?*

Kid: *not at all. See you at dark.*

Ben Slick was a hillbilly like everyone else the Kid knew. He was also an orator of sorts, and a backwoods philosopher. Every now and then he'd quote Socrates or Kant. Everyone who knew him said he was full of shit, but the Kid wasn't so sure. One time when he delivered the newspaper, the Kid caught him studying a philosophy book on his back porch. The Kid figured he had his doctorate in reading the moon phases, watching people, judging a good dog. Ben Slick knew the Kid's father had a reason for naming that red foxhound Scrip, and meant to find out what it was. He would get his answer tonight.

Darkness came. Stars studded the sky like the glass diamonds on Ole Scrip's collar. Silver moonlight fringed the mountains of coal. Ben Slick, the Kid and the Kid's dad walked into the night together and cast Scrip to the hills. Off in the distance, they heard his beautiful tenor bawl as he struck the scent of fox: baaaaaahhoooOOOooo! Then came the chase and more mountain music, Scrip's blood telling him what to do.

Ben Slick: *why do you call him Scrip?*

The Kid's Dad: *I call him that because I want him to be a reminder to me that this boy here with us tonight, my boy, will never work in the coal mines. I made him promise he wouldn't. I know it's in his blood to mine coal, just as it's in that dog's blood to chase fox, bred into him. The coal mining in my family, even though we've done it for generations, will end with me. Every time I look at Scrip, call his name, or hear his voice off in the distance, it reminds me of my goal of having my son leave this area, go to a better place, a more fulfilling life. He will use his mind instead of his body to make a living.*

Ben Slick: *admirable, but what about his soul? We both know he has the soul of a coal miner, the soul of the Appalachians. Can he be happy in a new place?*

The Kid's Dad: *listen to that sound, Ben Slick.*

Ben Slick: *yes, it's beautiful!*

The Kid's Dad: *Ben, I want my son to be free, not a slave to coal.*

Franz Liszt's Czardas Music

for piano and violin livened the stage next to the bar
    while a Bohemian woman with two right brains and gypsy dress

snapped the fluid fingers of her two left hands across a calculator,
    computing songs danced, dances sang and liquor not consumed.

She then twisted and twirled inside her dress in a foreign tongue that
    sounded Slovak and danced the czardas with her two left feet. As
        she did,

the fourteen-year-old Kid, the grinning piano player, lined
        his empty whiskey
    shot glasses on the upright piano top, he too singing songs in Slovak,

stomping and stumbling with his foreign tongue until he fell
        off the stage
    and lay there grinning, grinning, grinning

when Eddie Gdula, the band director, pulled him up by his
    gaudy suspenders and carried him home, dumped him on the floor

of the spinning, empty room next to the dream of his mother's piano
    where he practiced his czardas and polkas. He slept there,

awakened to birds chirping in Slovak, dancing the czardas and polkas
    to the music he had played the night before.

The Kid picked himself up, danced and sang
    with the birds until all his foreign singing and dancing

was used up. Then he went on with his life, never again to dance or sing
in Slovak. Though he searched everywhere, he couldn't find

the gypsy woman with the two right brains who sang so lovely
and danced so lively, recording the czardas, polkas, and whiskey

not consumed in his life when he had been too young to play piano
and sing on the stage at the bar with Eddie Gdula's
Bohemian Band,

although once, when much older, he kissed someone like her
on the Charles Bridge in Prague.

Fastest Man in the Coal Country

Gravel kicked back into faces in the crowd as the starter screamed *race on* to the contenders. The two runners jumped off the starting line low and fast, slinging their weight in front of them to lighten their loads, both grunting, farting, jugular veins distended, eyes bugged, faces pressed back by speed, every muscle flexed and spurting adrenalin. The race between the ages in Midway had officially begun.

They had chosen the mostly level and straight Center Street in a town of only three streets for the runoff between Stosh, the redheaded, freckle-faced daredevil who had just won the Ohio Valley Athletic Conference track title for the 440 yard dash, and a forty-two-year-old coal miner who had been a running back with the claim to fame of playing football against Lou *The Toe* Groza at Martins Ferry High School. My father was long and fast for a short distance.

Everyone in the town of forty houses lined the street: the Zavackys, Gareks, Sclinichkas, Troyanovichs, Klouskys, Skirtichs, Micks, Pramicks, Gdulas and Gamciks. The challenge had been made in the Midway Co-op Store the day after Stosh won the conference title. Ben Slick bellowed that the red-headed teenager wasn't even the fastest man in town, let alone the area. He said Don Graham was faster, even at forty-two. Don said he was too old to run a 440, so a distance of 100 yards was agreed upon by both contestants, now digging into the tar-covered gravel on Center Street with the balls of their feet. The redhead felt there was no way he could lose.

The race was a virtual tie from start to finish, but the old man, my father, lunged at the end, nearly blowing a gasket, and was dubbed the winner by Mayor Ben, who had been stirring up interest in the race for a week by blowing the political smoke of tall tales and outright lies in the town's clubhouse. Just as he crossed the finish line, my dad grabbed his hamstring. His entire right leg turned blue for a month, and he hobbled all summer. The doctor said he'd torn the muscle in half, lucky he hadn't herniated himself as well, but he was crowned fastest man in the coal country of Belmont County.

Sunday Night Entertainments

Sunday night in Appalachia brought a halt to the great earth movers that in one bite could lift the equivalent of six standard carloads of dirt and rock from the side of a mountain to get at the bituminous coal beneath. Momentarily stopped, too, the coal cutters that chewed up four-foot veins of anthracite, hauled out of holes in the earth a quarter mile deep and spit into railroad cars. Sunday night was for gathering, laughing together, sharing popcorn and Pepsi Cola while watching the first TV in town in George Skrtich's living room.

George Skrtich, a boss in the mine, made a little more money than everyone else, thus bought Midway's first television set in 1954. On that Sunday night ten years later when Ed Sullivan hosted the Beatles for the first time in America, sixty people, including Ben Slick and the Kid, packed themselves into one room with a black and white, sixteen-inch Sylvania. Screaming could be heard coming from the Skrtich's home as coal miners' daughters went wild, dancing, gyrating, popcorn spilling, thrilling the hills with shaking mountain fever. Afterwards, everyone stood in line to use the first indoor-toilet facility in town, just across the alley at Don Graham's house. He was the mine mechanic who knew carpentry, hydraulics, electricity and plumbing as well as how to fix a broken coal cutter. He'd rigged the toilet, made people think he was some kind of engineer genius. People were nearly as excited to hear the swoosh and swirl of gurgling suck of the flush as they were to listen to the Beatles.

Anyone who worked hard could eat popcorn and watch the Beatles on Sunday night in the Skrtich's living room, then walk across the alley to flush the commode, listen to water disappear into pipes that ran into the underground to be cleansed by tree roots, filtered by strata of rock, and washed away, reaching the mine shafts, then on to those great networks that led to the sea where molecules of clear water from the

Appalachians were lifted skyward by swirling winds drifting upward, suspended in the vast enigma of space, mixing the water of Appalachia with all the other waters of the world. Yes, Ben Slick, the Kid and all the others heard every bit of this in the sound of that first flush in the night as . . . *and I been workin' like a dog* rocked the air across the alley.

Dynamite Man

Kaboom! The cakewalk in the coal town came to an abrupt halt. The playing of Eddie Gdula's Polka Band stopped. Another blast! The crowd looked about, then at each other in wonderment. When the smoke dispersed, a bloody left hand was revealed, followed by a scream of terror heard above the merriment of the annual Midway Labor Day Festival and Cakewalk. Dick Danecki had played the game of chicken, making a five-dollar bet with another ball player from a rival town to see who could hold their M-80 firecracker longer. His exploded before he released it, causing him to lose two fingers off his left hand, the one the star pitcher, a southpaw, used to grasp a baseball. The scream coming from Danecki as he looked down at his hand was the scream of a slave as the whip came down across his back. Ben Slick explained to the Kid his outcry was not so much from physical pain as the stark realization that his promising life in baseball was gone with those fingers, blown away. His nasty curveball would be no more. Now he would be a coal miner.

The people, gathered together from nearby coal towns, resumed the horseshoe tournament and the dancing around the circle that had been roped off and designated the cakewalk area. This time the music stopped as planned. Another lucky winner. Standing closest to the number written on a cardboard sign dangling from a rope that matched the number drawn from a hat, the Kid was awarded a tasty cake fresh from the oven. Ice-cold, frothy beer was again drawn from the keg. The party continued after the brief interlude caused by the exploding firecracker.

Dick Danecki returned from the hospital later that night. Stumps were fashioned from the mess the firecracker made of the third and fourth fingers on his throwing hand. The party was over. People returned to their homes to rest before going back to the mines the following day.

The Kid took home the cake he'd won at the cakewalk. Alone, Danecki did his best to drain the keg. He worked at it diligently for the rest of the night, for the remainder of his life. After his hand healed, he resumed playing local baseball. He lost 10 miles per hour off his fastball. His curve hung in the air, suspended like a scream in a nightmare. He got a job in the coal fields of Belmont County, worked with explosives as a detonator, a dynamite man. In years to come, Ben Slick would watch Danecki play in the Twilight League, watch the left hander with missing fingers hang his curveball and get plastered every night.

Communion Underground

Smoke chugged from stacks at Wheeling Steel, drifted along the river above coke ovens and towns in the coal fields; the Ohio Valley filled with gray—everything: buildings, streets, supply yards, even the faces and lungs of people—dirty. Some days, if there was smog, everyone coughed, and eyes burned from sulfur and soot—the filth both seen and unseen.

Sunday morning at a whorehouse. Most regular people in church. Two plumbers—the Kid and Harry Bomshakner—hacked in the early morning smog as they donned their hardhats, strained to lift the heavy cover off a manhole in front of the busy hotel on Main Street in downtown Wheeling, then pushed a ladder down to look into the sewer. Anticipating an ordinary day of setting out MEN WORKING signs and clearing drains, the Kid peered into the tunnel. To him, it was like looking down the mineshaft at Willow Grove where his family worked. He descended into this black chasm of blind alleys and dead ends that was darker than night. He turned on his flashlight, slid the end of a metal snake into the confluence of concrete, steel and slime in the sewer ditch, that labyrinth of caverns and chasms, while his boss, Harry Bomshakner, started the motor on the snake auger unit up on the street beside the manhole, then stuck his head into the sewer and yelled: *Kid, what do you see down there?*

The Kid, a naive high school student trying to make an extra buck on the weekend as a plumber's helper, bellowed back as objects began to churn in the ditch with the snake: *empty bottles of Rolling Rock, one high-heeled shoe, handcuffs, a black bra and underwear, a Slovak prayer book, and enough used condoms to fill that empty peck basket you keep in your truck bed.* Rats scurried. Roaches punctuated the seediness that occurred in the hotel now confessing its sins in the stench of the dark below—a communion underground. A timeless place, land of the dead, always night, the sewer channel was infused with dirty blood running in the vein of a river under the city. Then from the deep, the Kid heard the echo of a scream—AAAAAAH!—without having heard its source, as if someone had answered him without his having asked. He wiped the sweat from his forehead and bellowed again: *let me outta here!*

Harry Bomshakner had a contract with owners of the old brick hotel, famous as a hooker establishment in the 1950s and '60s. Agreeing to keep the sewer lines open, he went there many times. In a whorehouse, people were always flushing items they shouldn't down the toilet, like underwear and condoms. This time Harry and the Kid would have to go inside the hotel from an entrance on the side street, as there appeared to be two clogs, one in the main sewer line beneath the street and another proximal to the main line up in the hotel. On this Sunday, they would be investigating room to room until the problem was identified.

As the Kid and Harry accessed the hotel's side entrance and walked up a dirty wooden staircase, they could hear laughter from the rooms as if it were still Saturday night. Then the faint sound of a scream—aaaaaah!—reverberated down the dimly lit corridor as they climbed the trash-littered stairs. Harry kicked a dead rat to the side. Smeared lipstick graffitied walls with cursive *Jesus Saves, Peace and F___ You(s)!* A pair of black panties hung limply from a potted plant on the first landing. A picture of a woman with a black parasol, dancing naked in sunlight, hung on the wall. The Kid wondered who the artist was, and even more, who was the woman. They knocked on several doors. Almost everyone who answered (even some of the men) wore black lingerie like the bra floating in the sewer. The place reeked of stale booze, the stench worse than the sewer.

Finally, the clogged drain was located. One of the women had flushed her belongings down the toilet in disgust after learning her best friend, another prostitute and former high school classmate who attended the same Orthodox church, died in the hotel that night. The two workers boot-sloshed through stagnant water covering the bathroom floor, inserted a snake and opened the line. After it cleared, the Kid went back to the street, climbed into the sewer to see what pushed through. The culprit: a black mink stole mingling with the underwear, empty bottles and prayer book with the golden Orthodox cross inscribed on its cover.

The dead woman's friend had found her handcuffed, suspended from a brass, wall-mounted coat hanger by a black leather belt in the room adjacent to the one where the plumbers worked. Later, the Kid would comment to Harry: *that scream we heard in the hallway while we were climbing the staircase—I wonder who made it? I also heard it when I was down in the sewer.*

The hanged woman's friend and coworker squinted, and her eyes burned in the smog as she walked out of the hotel into the light of day. She cringed from the loud clang as the men dropped the cover back on the manhole. It reverberated in her ears like the single peel of a church bell. As the plumbers loaded their signs and equipment into the truck, she asked them for a ride to the Orthodox cathedral at the edge of town, said she was going to hitchhike back to her family farm on the outskirts of Cleveland. Said she was tired of coal miners and steel workers with their rough hands and foul language. Said she planned to go back to school, become a teacher, first grade, wanted to get to the kids before their lives were tainted, dirtied. She said she wanted them fresh like morning sunlight.

After the Kid and Harry drove her to the edge of town, she slipped out of the truck, told them goodbye. As they motored away, the Kid looked back in the mirror to see her holding a black parasol and prayer book, sunlight streaming through her sheer dress, illuminating the outline of her slim legs and thighs. She blew the Kid a kiss then swept her tongue across her lips. The Kid wondered: *did she know at this moment she had almost died for lack of love? Could she morph into a new self, her secret life hidden like something moving beneath the city, the Ohio River flushing the screams of Wheeling whores from sewers into the underworld?*

Bone Crusher

Friday night. Game night. We were at their place. The stands packed. Two undefeated arch rivals: the Martins Ferry Purple Riders vs. the St. Clairsville Red Devils for the Ohio Valley Athletic Conference high school football championship. A hard-hitting nail-biter and head-banger. By halftime, Bone Crusher, Ferry's famed middle linebacker, had racked up his usual number of orthopedic injuries on our team: a broken arm and swollen knee, a fractured nose, dislocated shoulder. Somehow, I managed not to be among the disabled going into the fourth quarter. We were down 7-6 by a missed Bone Crusher-blocked extra-point kick. One minute left. Our defense held. 'Ferry had to punt. We got the ball back on our own 40-yard line, good enough field position for a late score. Two running attempts failed. Third and 10. I was supposedly the possession receiver, the big third-down guy, the guy who moved the chains. No touchdowns, just move the chains. Coach Higgenbotham called my number in a crossing pattern down the middle of the field, which, if completed, would give us a 15-yard pick-up and first down. The play had worked many times that season. Only one problem: I was to run right into the teeth of the defense, into the chomping jaws of the Bone Crusher, 225 pounds of Wheeling Steel. People from my hometown were thinking and saying things like: *Kid, Bone Crusher is going to rearrange your face, chew you a new butthole, put casts on your arms and legs!*

The ball left the hand of our strong-armed quarterback as a spiraling missile, heat seeking: sizzling, sizzling, sizzling through air, making the stadium lights brighten. It struck my hands flaming hot. Just as I began to tuck the ball away to secure the catch, there he was, that animal, Bone Crusher, bearing down on me like a man-eating rhino: *orrraaahhhh, immmaaahhh, eaaatyouuuuu!* His helmet struck me hard in the chest, right where the ball was placed, his hit timed perfectly.

My sternum crunched, then whimpered. My neck snapped my helmet off. One shoe flew to the right, the other to the left. My jock strap tangled around my shoulders. My mouth guard jammed into my eyeball. The lights dimmed. The sound went out. And the ball . . . well, it shot straight up end-over-end, came down into the waiting arms of Bone Crusher who raced for the end zone. His teammates pancaked two would-be tacklers. Bone Crusher ate the rest of our team alive: free and clear, he picked up steam, crossed the 20-yard line, the 10, the 5; then flamed into the end zone. He knocked down the goal posts, ran into the parking lot, flipped our team bus onto its side, tore a tire off, took a bite out like it was a chocolate donut. He kept on running right into the Ohio River, through the Wheeling Tunnel and beyond, into the fields of the sky.

As for me, well, they took me for reconstructive surgery, put in a new breast plate, reattached my arms and legs, rewired my backbone to my brain, took my butt off my face, dumped all the chicken parts out of my head and screwed it back into the hole at the top of my spine. After extensive rehab I was finally able to walk again, albeit with the same hitch I have in my gait today. I still make grimacing faces and babble a bit on occasion: *blub, blub . . . blab, blab*—sometimes cock my head to the side and drool when asked what happened that night in early November of 1964 down on the Ohio River when the Purple Riders rode our butts into the ground, stomped on our shish kabobs, stole our pride and joy, and sent us home to our mommies and daddies to cry.

Looming

A loom in the loft of the barn today rests idle in the sweet smell of hay. Worn-out garments, bed sheets, torn shirts and blouses were collected and carried to the barn for looming. Baskets of rags, cut and tied into long narrow strips, were reeled into balls unrolled at the loom, then warped, shuttled and woven into rugs. On Sunday afternoons, the Kid often watched his grandmother and Veronica Pulcask, two elderly Slovak women, perform their magic with rags. They stood each to a side, slamming cloth together on the five-foot wooden loom that churned out rag rug after rag rug to sell at the market in town. Those patternless arrangements of cloth and color, placed on doorsteps and living room floors, earned cash that put food on our table. While the weavers worked high in the loft, below them cows in their stanchions ground mouthfuls of hay to the shuttling rhythm of the loom.

A Holy Night

Fall on your knees! O hear the angels' voices! O night divine. O night when Christ was born. O night divine . . .

The powerful singing of the coal miner made the Midway clubhouse walls reverberate, giving voice to the town. The Kid began to discern it as he walked toward the sound, a humming from afar, distinct as he drew closer. Late for Christmas-caroling practice. Friday night. He had to hitchhike home that late November evening of 1964, finishing work at his after-school job with Porterfield's Furniture in St. Clairsville. This would be the Kid's last Christmas of singing carols with the towns-people as they walked from house to house behind the piano loaded on the back of music conductor, Andy Hobart's pickup truck, with Bingo Mriz and his wad of chewing tobacco dressed as the jolly Santa riding shotgun with bags of candy and nuts for the children. On the porch of the clubhouse, leaning back on his chair against the wall, sat Ben Slick, nursing a brown bottle of Carling Black Label, his eyes entranced by moonlight as if carried away by the sound of "O Holy Night." The Kid startled him when his foot creaked the porch boards.

Ben Slick: *hey Kid, you're late. Your old man is really hitting the high notes tonight. His voice is something, isn't it?*

Realizing he was in for a Ben Slick monologue, the Kid answered: *yes, it is. He makes the walls of this old shack seem strong when they come alive with sound.*

Ben Slick: *it is powerful. It's the true voice of our town. You know he's singing for all the miners who died in Willow Grove. Their wives and children are all in there, singing with your dad, some of them weeping, still crying for their men. The song "O Holy Night" brings it out. That's the beauty of the Christmas caroling we have here. It lets us remember our past, and yet, give gifts to the future of our little town, the children.*

Then: *I suppose this will be your last Christmas here, Kid. You're going on to college, a beautiful thing. You're breaking away from the tradition of working in the coal mines. Your dad taught you well. He showed you the way out. We'll miss you. Many of us are old. We might not be here when you come back, if you ever do.*

Kid: *I'll be back. Probably be home for Christmas next year. I get holidays off, you know.*

Ben Slick: *yes, but sometimes things change,* thinking: *life can take some unusual turns at times.* He says: *the Vietnam war is in high gear. The lady up at the Selective Service Office in St. Clairsville, Milly Tisko, is committed to getting Midway boys called to serve. She said our town has been underrepresented in the war. I say we paid our dues at Willow Grove. I'll pray for you, Kid, pray you don't get drafted to go over there. I cringe when I watch the body counts on the six o'clock news. They call it a conflict! My ass! So many of this country's young boys are needlessly dying. Stay in school, Kid. Study and play football. Hold on to that II-S deferment for as long as you can. I'm a WWII Veteran, but I wouldn't look down on you if you went to Canada. I just don't believe in this war. If you do get called, go to the skies and aviation. Fly! That's what your dad and I did in WWII, but that was a different time. We felt justified in fighting for our country, for freedom. Vietnam has nothing to do with freedom for us. It's all politics as far as I'm concerned.*

Kid: *I'll be back! I promise you.*

The Kid opened the door to the clubhouse. It came back at him when the whoosh of sound struck him in the face like the whoosh of explosion coming from the mine tunnel at Willow Grove, only much softer and without the afterdamp. He took his place in the town choir, and like a canary, began to sing, his voice blending in with the others: *the thrill of hope, the weary world rejoices, for yonder breaks a new and glorious morn . . .*

The Exception

She might have said something like: *hey, sailor, over here!* He might have gazed into those eyes, green behind auburn hair, and rather than hello, his first words: *dinner tonight, Georgetown?* She might have replied: *I don't go out with sailors, but for you I might make an exception.* At an Italian restaurant in Georgetown, they shared a glass of wine. Then after dinner, on the street, he might have push-started his blue VW bug, expertly popping the clutch to start the engine, playing the emergency-brake handle like a cello. She might have laughed, even said: *I have never been on such a cheap date,* paused, then added: *I might like to spend more time with you—intimate time.* He swallowed hard. Then she might have hesitated again, saying: *aren't you curious why?* He might have smartly answered: *because I'm so good looking?* Giggling, her reply: *no, I like the way you play the handle on your brake, like a bass player at the Kennedy Center. I can't believe you drive in D.C. with a dead battery and no brakes! I think you might be crazy! You sailors aren't paid nearly enough! How was a penniless person like you ever assigned to work for my boss, Bill Lukash, Nixon's doctor?*

He might have liked hearing that. Then she might have heard him say: *let's go for ice cream!* She might have laughed again and said: *I suppose next you'll want to meet my parents!* He might have liked the way she licked her cold spoon. Upon meeting her parents, her father muttered: *oh no, a young man from Appalachia, and a sailor! You're in for a wild ride! I told you never to bring a bluejacket here!* Then, she might have taken him home, to her real home, the one with the bedroom. She might have even smiled a body of freckles at him—her skin dappled like a filly at the track. And they might have ridden the outer edge of the oval, to get the longest ride possible. No winning or losing here; no race to finish. It might have been love. He might have been the exception. She might have been the exception. Years later (and it seemed like a hundred) he looked back on it, thought to himself: *you know, it's been a good ride, all in all.* Then, he wrote it down, along with the other stories, and read it aloud somewhere. He just might have been naïve-crazy enough to do that. It was a crazy time: Woodstock, The Age of Aquarius, Jimi Hendricks, Martin Luther King, Jr., the draft, body counts, Vietnam. Did it really happen, or was it imagined? At this point, does it matter? Nothing matters now except for love, and love might have been the only thing that ever mattered.

First Solo

Sioux Falls One Seven Six, wave off . . . wave off!—the cockpit radio ratcheted orders from the control tower—to me, a Navy Ensign in training, flying Sioux Falls #176 on my first solo flight. What could possibly be wrong? Only ten feet from touchdown, my landing attempt felt right. I waved off, gave the Beechcraft T-34B full throttle, hard left rudder into the crosswind. As I pulled the stick back and landing gear up, I thought I heard the voice of my grandmother's broken English/Slovak dialect speaking to me from her porch, fading in and out like a radio: *Janka, you no [kssh . . . kssh] fly aeroplane. Stay here on land with me. It safe here. You no [kssh . . . kssh] leave me. I die if you leave me.* Then again, the real radio with its own static: *Sioux Falls One Seven Six, you had your [kssh . . . kssh] flaps down! This is a no flap day!*

Whew! Thank God it was a technicality, not something structural. When the wind speed was greater than fifteen knots, flaps were not permitted, as they were designed to catch wind, slow and soften the landing. High crosswinds could cause the aircraft to drift sideways if flaps were down, make it strike the runway off kilter, possibly flip and crash.

As I climbed back to 500 feet, aligning the tip of my wing to the end of the runway, I began re-circling in the landing pattern at the US Navy's Cradle of Aviation, now filled with clones of myself, scores of other student aviators out for their first solos. Every one of us a neophyte, uncertain and a little scared. We all felt the same anxieties and fears of making mistakes (like using flaps on a no-flap day or worse yet—crashing) on that windy March morning in the sunlight of Pensacola, Florida's Saufley Field.

From the cockpit, I looked down at the landing strip for Lt. Mike Bell, my flight instructor. I hoped he might be standing at the edge of the runway, waving up at me, a signal that I was alone, that he had supreme confidence in me, just as he had after I dropped him off during my safe-for-solo check flight the previous day. The thought of him being there gave me the courage to fly and land my aircraft unassisted, knowing he was standing by to watch me maneuver that hunk of red and white painted aluminum safely home. This time, though, except for a straight-out windsock, I was totally alone, my flight instructor already with another student, the process grinding forward, itself a big flying machine. What a feeling to be a part of the sky, engine humming, propeller awhir, the body of the aircraft buffeting rhythmically, a pulsating heart giving life to a dream.

I brought my trainer back around for another landing attempt, locked the wheels down, kept the flaps up this time, guided as if I were a kite on a string being pulled to the ground by the teaching of my instructor. My wheels kissed the runway, fitting the plane's center of gravity precisely into the earth's. The embrace of my touchdown with warm asphalt never felt so good, like flesh and blood relatives reunited after too much time apart, my cloud-soul into the ground-soul of my grandmother. The 100 minutes I flew solo were by far the longest time I'd ever been truly alone—perhaps, the only time.

In the air the minutes passed as if I'd lived another lifetime in another dimension.

Later, I would realize the aloneness wasn't aloneness at all, but a closeness so close to aloneness it was more about the satisfaction of overcoming an innate fear of failure and acquiring the lifelong attribute of self-confidence, something I'd earned—alone.

Silent Interview

As I sat in the chair next to her desk
casually chatting with her,
the tan young woman with no gold band
suddenly became quiet, stared
into my eyes and said: *you can
go in now. The doctor will see you.*
I strode into his office, the famous
aging transplant surgeon with both feet
propped on a wooden desk, his skilled
left hand with its plain gold band
holding my application for medical school.
He sported the same tan
as his young ringless secretary.
Intuition told she was his mistress,
that they had vacationed in the winter sun
on precisely the same Caribbean beach,
made love for a week on the sand?
For the interview, he wore brown
leather cowboy boots, shit kickers.
He stared at me, standing there
in front of him for what seemed like at least
the time it took for him and his lover
to ravish each other, their tans the only thing
to give them away. After looking me over,
he spoke:
*Jesus, son, you've got quite an application
here! Top test scores, and you aced everything.
How'd you do it? Busted your butt, that's how.
I know. And your old man's a coal miner!*

You must be one tough SOB! This profession
needs solid, hard-working doctors.
You won't put up with nonsense from anybody,
that's for sure, not with this pedigree. And
at the same time, you'll display compassion.
We will take you here, in Charleston,
and you'll come. Why? Because you need
this place, that's why. You need its culture,
and you'll get an excellent medical education.
We're the second oldest school in the country
and the first in the South. Oh, other places will
want you, but you'll come here. Good luck
to you! You'll make it, son!

That was my interview
at the Medical University of South Carolina.
The tall surgeon didn't bother
to find out if I could speak.
He stood up. We shook hands.
In a refined manner, he pointed to the door.
His secretary smiled as I walked out.
She followed me with her complicated eyes
as if to say: *I'm the one who told him*
to take you! I placed your application
on the top of his pile.

The Thump

Kid, summoned his calm but concerned wife, seated at the table with their two toddlers directly across from him: *the man behind you just put his face down in his mashed potatoes!* The doctor emergent in the Kid turned toward him, pulled the man's head out of the smothering potato goo, cleared his airway, checked for a pulse and finding none took a fist and smacked him in the middle of his chest. The hard precordial thump reignited the man's internal furnace. He sucked air like it was the first breath out of his mother's womb, then blurted: *where am I?*

Kid: *you're at Mehlman's in St. Clairsville.*

Old man: *what day is it?*

Kid: *it's Sunday after church.*

Old man: *what happened?*

Kid: *you briefly died, but now you're okay.*

The old man's friends congratulated each other for his life having been saved by a miracle. Meanwhile a physician, dressed like a woodcutter on his day off in a flannel shirt and blue jeans, attended to him on the floor until the ambulance came. Then he attended to his unfinished piece of homemade lemon meringue pie, gathered up his young family and hurried into the bright light of afternoon. He had been searching for weeks for an answer to his dilemma of deciding whether or not to take over a retiring doctor's private practice or enter the field of Emergency Medicine. On a rare day off, he took his family back home, to the coal fields, to look through the wreckage for the answer.

As the family of four walked out of Mehlman's Cafeteria, the Kid's wife thumped him with this revelation: *did you notice that no one thanked you for saving that man's life? For some reason, his friends thanked each other instead. They had no idea you were a doctor. You didn't tell them you were. Do you think people actually deserve to have a physician on call 24/7 to cater to their every whim?*

The Kid's answer: silence for several days. Then he declined the offer made by Lee Underwood, the prominent, retiring physician in Canton, Ohio, and entered the field of Emergency Medicine, enjoying a rewarding family life as well as the privilege of snatching people directly from the thick mashed-potato goo of death every day, saving one after the other for thirty years.

"One Fainting Strand of Spiderweb"

Kaboom! The last shot fired. The Kid had come back to hear the 21-gun salute at the cemetery on Memorial Day, its parade always ending at the graveyard. When he was younger, he attended this event with his father, a WWII veteran. Now he was the veteran honoring the graves of his family: his father next to his mother, not far from her parents and his father's mother. All were laid to rest young, after cancer took them down. All gone in three years.

Parade over, the kid made the short drive to his old hometown, Midway, to see how much had changed. He found houses razed, others dilapidated. Overall, the town less tidy than he remembered. He didn't see anyone he recognized. All new faces. As he drove past Ben Slick's home, he noticed a red dog in the yard that looked just like Scrip, the foxhound of his youth. The Kid stopped, slipped out of his truck to pet him, the dog acting as though he knew him. Then a voice came from the porch.

Nurse: *can I help you?*

Kid: *I used to live in this town.*

Nurse: *there's no one left from the old days.*

Kid: *what about Ben Slick? Is he still alive?*

Nurse: *yes, but barely.*

Kid: *how old is he now?*

Nurse: *ninety-nine.*

Kid: *can I see him?*

Nurse: *certainly. He hasn't had a visitor in quite some time. He had a stroke, you know. It affected his vision. He's nearly blind, able to see only forms and movement.*

Kid: *how's his mind?*

Nurse: *rather perfect, I'd say.*

As they walked into Ben Slick's room, the Kid noticed a stack of books on the table. He recognized *To a Blossoming Pear Tree* by poet James Wright, as the Kid's writing professor in South Carolina, James Dickey, once read a poem of Wright's aloud to the class. He also knew Ben Slick had attended the annual James Wright Poetry Festival in Martins Ferry. As the nurse picked up Immanuel Kant's book, *Perpetual Peace,* she quietly explained that Ben Slick had her read to him several hours each day. Her voice, a whisper, awakened the self-appointed town mayor.

Ben Slick: *who's there? I see three forms.*

Kid: *it's me, Ben Slick, the Kid.*

Ben Slick: *oh, why yes, certainly, son. Did you come back to heal me, doctor? I'm beyond saving now. I hear you found a farm to live on and call it Lone Willow? I get news of you from time to time from your godmother, Rosalie Troyanovich, in New Athens.*

Kid: *yes, I did find a farm, and came home for the Memorial Day Festival in St. Clairsville.*

Ben Slick: *thank you for honoring the WWII veterans like myself. I'm the only one left in this town. In fact, I'm the only person still here from the days when you lived here. Everyone's died or moved away now that the coal is gone.*

Kid: *it's sad, isn't it?*

Ben Slick: *yes, it is, somewhat, but when I think of the success stories of the youth of this town, it gives me great joy. This little coal town of forty houses produced an aerospace engineer for NASA, a metallurgist and Executive VP for Caterpillar, a doctor, two schoolteachers and a nurse. Quite an accomplishment, I'd say! Did you know that out of the thirty students in your eighth-grade class at Wheeling Township School in Fairpoint, twenty-five went on to college degrees?*

Kid: *no, I wasn't aware of that.*

Ben Slick: *yes, that fact alone gives me a feeling of accomplishment and peace, like my time here on earth wasn't wasted. Your teachers, Ms. Warnock, Mr. Reed, Mr. Wilkins and the others, did a commendable job. Of course, your big break in life came when you were selected to work for The White House physician while stationed at Bethesda Naval Medical Center, opening some doors that otherwise might never have been available to you.*

Ben Slick dropped his glasses to the floor, then continued: *now it's time for me to rest, son. You must leave me to myself, but before you go, please read me a poem from James Wright, another local product made good. Not many around here even know of him. Poets often don't get the recognition they deserve.*

Kid: *I'd be honored to read to you.*

Ben Slick closed his eyes, drifted away in peace as the Kid read "On a Phrase from Southern Ohio," a poem by James Wright, a standing recitation just as he had done in grade school:

> *. . . and still in my dreams I sway like one fainting strand*
> *of spiderweb, glittering and vanishing and frail*
> *above the river.*

As the Kid closed the book to walk away, a paper fell from it, written in the hand of Ben Slick, saying:

> *These are my wishes now: a 21-gun salute,*
> *bagpipes playing, a foxhound baying off in the*
> *distance from the other side of the mountain.*
> *Can you see to it? There is no one else.*

Two forms walked away from Ben Slick's room, leaving the third to linger awhile, looming, reading to him in silence.

III.

Black Lung

He came out of an Appalachian coal mine the way a fighting cock
    might strut from a coop after a skirmish,
feathers tarnished but still sporting an attitude, the way Cassius Clay
    did before he became Ali.

He came out of an Appalachian coal mine clawing and crawling,
    the way a ghost crab
    might move across sand on some long-ago beach once traveled
on the Black Sea as he emigrated from the dark side of a sunray.

He came out of an Appalachian coal mine angry, fighting the stink
    of sulfur soot
in air that had lost its promise, spitting out tiny black spots in the snow
    from beaded alveoli huddled together
like a family staring at a chest radiograph that hung from a view box
    in a hospital room in Martins Ferry,
the doctor going on and on about my grandfather's black lung disease.

He came out of an Appalachian coal mine, heaped onto an anonymous
    burning slag pile
like all the other men who carry hollow metal lunch pails and crawl
    from mines.
They drag their dust-filled lungs, cough up phlegm, black
    like radiographic crows that roost
in branches of barren winter trees, their silhouettes *caw, caw, cawing*
    until, one by one, they plummet to the ground.

Black Lung Money

I

At home at 60, my grandfather coughed up red phlegm flecked
    black with coal dust,
then frank blood into a white towel. Lips pursed, basically
    already planted,
he breathed through an imaginary straw for the balance of his life,
    sticking the tube up through dust like a periscope.
The doctor told him it was pneumoconiosis. None of us knew
    what that meant, though we heard
he would get a pension for it—black lung money. Of course,
    he also smoked
four packs of Lucky Strikes daily. I never knew him without one.
    The pension money was not refused.

II

At the cemetery, before he was lowered, thunder rumbled,
    a subterranean whoosh.
The earth shook for an instant as if dynamited, or was it
    an explosion of methane in a mine tunnel.
Who knows for certain what goes on when you're underground.
    It began to rain.
Umbrellas opened—black lungs expanding. A prayer was said.
    The rain stopped—
umbrellas closed—solemn exhalations.

III

At parties, he was a polka dancer, swiller of port, baseball
    aficionado with the nickname "Shortstop."

Once, his great grandson, a shortstop, made an acrobatic catch
    of a ball that seemed as though it had been dropped
from the sky, the egg of a rare golden bird, and the catching of it
    saved an entire species from extinction.
The black lung checks kept coming in the mail to my grandmother
    though she never set foot underground:
the United Mine Workers' gesture to the remainder
    of the family.

After autopsy his lungs were immersed in formaldehyde,
    suspended in a pickle jar,
the family feeling this was right as he often went
    to the refrigerator
to drink pickle juice directly from a mason jar in the morning
    after getting pickled the night before.
His lungs on view were thought to save others in some remote,
    cold way after being studied
by medical students in a pathology lab like eggs of black gold
    preserved for all time.

Counting Rings

I. The Sawing of It

Sweat dripped from chins and foreheads, splashed on the long,
    shiny sawblade.
Drip, pull. Drip, pull. Muscles flexed, engorged, stiffened
    then relaxed.
My grandmother, carrying spring water, placed a hand
    on my spent twelve-year-old arm.
Cool, knobbed fingers whispered to my burning bicep
    taut under skin: *Janka, you strong like bull!*

My elderly grandfather, stationed opposite me, was the counter-puller
    reflected with the day moon
on the crosscut saw's crystal ball. I looked into its shine to see
    blue-tinged sweat dripping
off the counter-puller's chin whiskers onto the knotted rope
    of his arm,
his farmer's tan leaning into the halved apple tree, counting rings
    dropped to the ground after the storm.

II. Two Years Later This Blue Man

sat in the day moon of his wheel chair in the doorway to his room
    with his head thrown back,
long hair stiff, fanning away from him as if it wanted to go
    somewhere else.
His counting-rings leg of applewood and harness leather
    dropped to the floor.
Was he putting it on or taking it off? His stump wasn't sure
    or wouldn't tell

but sat with him, staring out, its end-pouch of loose skin aghast,
    open-mouthed.

Standing to the side was this blue man's best friend, his hand-made
    wooden walker with tricycle wheels
he'd fashioned to roll him to the dancing, polkas, the young women
    he'd twirl
in colorful patterns of hidden passion into various stages
    of rigor mortis.

The wooden walker, his loyal aide, escorted him to the co-op store
    for another pack of Lucky Strikes,
another pint of port, knowing he'd done it right, his way—
    a do-it-your-selfer,
maker of wooden legs and walkers was this blue man.

Our Porch

Thoughts of my grandmother and our porch come together as we sit side by side in my mind, flesh and blood touching, a strong branch holding onto the last apple of summer. A memory kindles when a contrapuntal dove calls from a fluted tree at morning's first light. In that light is the fragrance of dill drying, basil and parsley in baskets, lavender in bloom at our feet, bread baking fresh in the oven of a coal stove, visions of mushrooms and cut asters hanging in bunches at the door, tastes of carmelized apple pie bubbling with cinnamon, sounds of a hummingbird, its whir on a honeysuckle blossom.

On our porch we loved each other, Vera Troyanovich and I. She my Baba; I her Janka. One evening, sitting together, as we watched her flock of laying hens leap to catch fireflies before going to roost, we looked up to the roar of a low-flying aircraft and saw contrails from other planes crisscrossing the evening sky. She placed her hand on mine and said: *Janka, you no fly aeroplane. Stay here on ground with me. It safe here. You no leave me, Janka. We have farm, own land. It good here. You make me happy. I die if you leave me.*

I was drafted. Never promising I wouldn't, I flew airplanes. The branch let go of summer's last apple, falling away into the basket that rested on the worn wooden bench of our porch.

In the Sweet Time

Like a young teen's fascination with smoking his first stolen cigarette, the train tunnel from childhood looms in memory: distorted, a crooked picture plastered on a mountain of rock with tracks hanging off. In this dark opening, cut through veins of coal and sandstone at the base of a mountain, are four manholes, two on each side, carved into a wall only four feet away from the tracks. The holes are to be used if someone is in the tunnel when a train comes through.

I see four boys kneel to ground, fix their ears to tracks to listen—a locomotive can be detected a mile away. Once alerted, the boys run into the tunnel, fill the manholes, listen up close, first to the warning whistle then to the roar of the train, and see sparks fly, feel the heavy, violent jolting as wheels strike joints between long rails of steel.

They feel the earth shake. The train passes at full speed only four feet away in the tunnel. Intense pressure in their ears gives them the same nirvana that follows witnessing violent death, in this case potentially their own. They do it for kicks, just for the thrill, to see if a new initiate pisses himself out of fear of being sucked out of the shallow manhole by the force of the train and dies in the tunnel.

Afterward, the boys sit outside the tunnel on the trestle, fish for mud suckers in Wheeling Creek, drink hard cider and smoke cigarettes stolen from their fathers' secret stashes. I hear them laugh, carry on in the warm sunlight of an April Sunday afternoon. I hear them talk about the train, how they could have touched it by merely reaching out a hand if not paralyzed by fright. The boys are in the sweet time of their lives, before they are the ones who work in the mines, fill railroad cars with the black cargo trains carry to burn in mills downriver, making the Ohio Valley choke, stagger onto its face, fall and piss itself into a permanent, polluted sleep.

Message Home

. . . and my letter arrived too late, long after everyone had already gone.

From here I feel you there
and understand your position.
Rather than dig coal as did seven
generations of men in our family
before me, I choose to analyze
its composition chemically and
psychologically, letting it lead me
to new places rather than enter
the great hole where you are now
to breathe its dust and have it
cover me up with you.
Academically speaking, I will
take another path into the ground.
I hope you understand as we both
know where my soul originated and
why this is so difficult for me to say:
I am the wolf who becomes
renegade, jumping the confines
of the world he was born into,
only to discover in the new
freedom another binding set
of circumstances even more
constrictive and suffocating than
those left behind. Regardless,
I do not want to participate
in another Willow Grove.

The Widow Maker

The man in question was tall, standing well over six feet.
He had to reach down more than most to get to the level of snow.

One year he made it through much of winter, then March came,
dumped a foot of heavy white. The man in question kept his place

in the country immaculate. He came home from a long day's work
as snowfall ended and began shoveling, first the walkways

then the driveway—to get the car out if need be. He leaned
into the job, reached down farther than most, the angle

afforded him greater than most. After shoveling, shoveling,
shoveling, he became ill, stopped to rest and light a Lucky Strike.

The smoke encircled his perspiring dome like a blue halo. The man
in question felt no better. His wife thought he had a sudden case
    of the flu.

She and their teenage daughters drove him to the hospital, miles away
through the snow. The ER doctor ran an EKG and muttered to himself:

tombstones! It's the widow maker all right, just as I suspected!
Horizontal now, on a flimsy gurney, the man in question

measured taller, still, than most, and his toes stood protuberantly blue
above the white sheets.

Winter's Tree: Elegy for My Father

Fallen as cold petals from winter's tree are stones upright on snow: the Apostles' Creed inscribed on one, your epitaph standing tall amongst other chiseled friends. The creed is a tribute to your dying young, unfinished, never seeing your grandchild hit a ball, shoot a basket, or your son, from the mountain of coal you took from the heart of the earth, become a doctor.

Or . . . maybe the inscription is placed there for the part you played in that Sunday mass. You were there for him when Father Kossi held up his arms in prayer, leaned back from the pulpit before the altar, gazed into the eyes of Jesus on the Cross, then suddenly collapsed, falling backwards into the congregation. No one knew what to do as he lay there, death in his face, without breath and still. But you, having taken that course in lifesaving for work in the mine, approached him as would a mechanic a fallen coal cutter. After checking his pulse and finding none, you performed CPR just as you had done to the what-proved-to-be practice priest manikin.

The coal from Father Kossi's mountain had been emptied from his heart. His fire cried out for reignition. You were the one chosen to put it back, relight the fire and save your priest, who thanked you two months later upon his return to mass that Sunday in Barton, Ohio's Saint Nicholas Russian Orthodox Church. Yes, you earned the creed on your stone. You lived it, believed in the one God who gathers the petals fallen from winter's tree, gives them the warmth of His hands, arranges them in rows in a basket of snow. Your son lingers awhile in the air with you. Together like cedar waxwings, you share fruit hanging from winter's tree.

In the Strange Dark Sky

Waiting for stars to gather 'round like white stones
          arranged in a jumbled pattern,
the moon hung tangentially in the black sky, lingered
          up there on a lonely street corner.
Stars held it all up, kept it from falling off sky's curb
          into the wobbly darkness.

From this very sky I pulled on a thread of string to find
          a long-ago kite
I'd left dangling by its tail from the top of a tall silver tree.
          Strange I should find it
in the dark like this. I remember flying it in the light
          of day in our backyard
while my mother nurtured her plot of zinnias and my brothers
          scrapped over a wiffleball game.

The place under the tree where my father parked his car
          was empty. Another tug on the string,
and the kite fell to the ground into that empty place.
          I went to it, discovered a ring of dark oil
in the pallid limestone, a black moon in a white sky—
          the reverse of the night I was dreaming in.

When my fingertip touched the dark spot, it felt thick
          like blood, warm and slick,
slipping away like something I couldn't remember—
          was it the Philadelphia Chromosome,
the genetic aberration linked to myeloid leukemia?

Oh yes, that was it, in the empty space where my father
            first taught me to fly a kite.
The story rests at an unusual angle in my mind, as if
            mathematically incongruent,
in a state of genetic improbability or denial, just as the moon
            was that night, hanging
tilted in the strange dark sky my mind had been living under.

Poet Above the River

for James Wright

As you hover above the river,
                    hummingbird on a honeysuckle vine
      leaning out over the steep bank
                of the Ohio at Martins Ferry,
   your memory fills spring
         with fragile sound and fragrance.

Gone are the smokestacks
            of Wheeling Steel, the deep
      earthen pits leaking orange
                into creeks, the virgin trees
   dying from acid rain.
         Now the land is healing,

its core replenished,
            lending solace
      as you dream from another place,
              sending the hummingbird
   to gather nectar
         in the silence of your words.

The Gentian-Spotted Star-Leaf Fell

On my walk through the fall woods that particular morning, the sky was the color of gentian. A single maple leaf fell from a treetop—up where the reds and yellows mingled with the purples and greens. When it touched the ground, it looked familiar, as if a star-shaped spot of gentian violet had been painted on its side. I swore the leaf was shaped and colored exactly like the one my small hand held up to her that particular morning, a leaf she took home to iron between two sheets of wax paper then place in a storybook.

Yesterday, grandson on my lap, I opened the book for the first time in two generations. The gentian-spotted star-leaf fell, preserved, to the floor, my namesake exclaiming: *look Grandpa, what came with the story! How did it get there?* The world quieted. I heard only her voice as she retold the fairytale of the Czech water spirit, Vodnik. The particular dress she wore that day the light watery green of a feed sack painted with gentian-flower eyes.

Only Shadows Live in Troll Town

No road led to Troll Town, its entrance blocked by an enormous slag pile. When the mine shut down, the vein of coal exhausted, people from the town moved to other places.

One summer, my father took me to Troll Town blackberry picking. I was just old enough to remember: about five. We had to wade Wheeling Creek, then climb a cliff wall to get there. The slag pile blocking the road burned from the inside out, smoldered for decades to form red dog gravel.

As we found our way to a crumbled sandstone foundation, once the basement of his home, Dad told me he was born in Troll Town in 1923. Nothing there now except stone, weeds and shadows, though I remember Dad telling me his memories were there—still in the shadows. He told a story from his childhood, a winter evening. A young woman in a feed-sack dress with no overcoat came to the door during a snowfall. Dad stood at the door, peering behind Elsie, his mother, to greet her. Barefoot and gloveless, the woman carried an empty metal can, asked to borrow kerosene for her lantern. Like the red dog hidden under snow, her feet were reddened. With his eyes, Dad walked her footprints back to their origin at the slag pile. He said she looked flawless standing on their porch with snowflakes in her auburn hair—an Irish, red dog angel from the slag heap by the creek.

Dad said even after he grew older and no longer lived in Troll Town, each time he passed the slag heap, embers glowed at its bottom and smoke from the top of the pile wafted into the sky. A warmth would come over him as though he was still at home on the porch of the coal shack, looking out at the red dog angel as she stood like a shadow in the snow. Once, he went by on a moonlit night and saw a lantern floating through trees on the hill where his house had stood—the Irish angel lighting her way through shadows in Troll Town.

Appalachia Healing

Ohio's Appalachian foothills ripple
onto each other to meet the sky, a beauty
forgiving even of the great earth movers,
the giant shovels with names
like Mountaineer and Gem of Egypt,
the bulldozers and haul trucks with no names
but manufactured by companies with names
like Caterpillar and Allis Chalmers,
and the coal companies owned by people
with names like Hanna and Rhodes, who raped
and pitted the land, left it for dead.
Those of us with local names like Mihalik
and Petro are responsible as well:
we drove the crawlers and great earth movers.

Despite years of abuse, repeated assaults,
warm sun and summer rain sprouted grassland,
undergrowth giving way to tall trees that covered
the land's wounds with layers of green.
This land made itself wild, composting
and renewing as it did before
the combustion engine, but not forgetting
or forgiving, forever looking over its shoulder
to see how it might happen again.

Hounds of Appalachia

Coursing on the wind like my mother's violin,
Appalachia plays her song for the old souls
who follow the hounds. Long-eared, silver-tongued
animals, blood-driven hunters, lean and swift,
the hounds race on, even with torn, padded feet.

Voices in the wind; forces of the wind; their quarry:
fox, bruin or cat, always ahead, wind-scented—
footprints in darkness followed. What begins excited,
joyful, becomes red flight on white snow.

They do what their instincts tell them. Their ears are heavy,
hear both what is on the wind and what is passed down
to them by the baying of ancestors in their blood.
They course the steep ridges and deep hollows
of foothills covering eons of smoldering dreams.

Bah-hoooOOOoooooooooo . . .

This is the way of the hound.
This is the way of the mountain.
This is the way of Appalachia
as it is now, as it was before.

Only the blooded hounds are witnesses and understand—
help us to know
what is on the land,
what is under the land,
what is above the land.

The story announces to the wind in the night, as the hounds
course the wooded ridgetops, settle into secluded hollows,
tell nothing but the sweet joyful truth—
explaining it all.

A nighthawk perched on a barren limb from a lookout
turns his head to the wind and soars, suspended in the story.

Listen: you too will hear it: the hounds of Appalachia,
coursing on the wind like my mother's violin.

Bah-hooOOOoooooooooo . . .

And when, at last, the hounds come in to you, get down
on all fours, ululate together, then let them lick each other and you
like sisters and brothers of wolves.

Thanksgiving

for James Dickey

Leaves fall at the speed of light.
The creek runs orange.
Thanksgiving.

Unearthed coal is slag-heaped;
sulfur diluted from it by rain—
acid leaching into the creek.

From within a tree left standing in pits of clay,
a death-stick drawn on a bow, missiles its way
through skin, ribcage, heart, ribcage and skin again.

The earth flows upward for an instant
into the big doe,
then brings her, crumpled, down to it.

The lone tree amidst unearthed rock and mud
drew her in for a final reunion of plant and animal.
Thanksgiving.

Her orange-mudded feet are cord-tied together.
She sways to and fro,
suspended from a horizontal tree-pole.

Feathers from the arrow protrude from her side.
Her head hangs cold.
Her tongue drips blood.

Two weary human frames carry her
from the orange, man-made mud-desert.
Blood mingles with unearthed coal and sulfur.

Tracks that she made coming in are walked over, obliterated.
A cigarette smolders in a hoofprint.
Thanksgiving.

Milkweed Seeds Stir in the Grasses

Oblong
became our shape
as we lay together
in the warm shadow of moonlight
on a spring night,
rain diluting our contours
into reproductive truth.
After fall's wind carried us for miles
from our follicles in fluffy white parachutes,
we were creatures from another world,
lifted over hills never before traveled.
You remember that night, don't you?
Milkweed seeds planted in darkness
camped the winter, waiting for sunlight
to spring forth our new forms
in the foothills of the Appalachians,
to emerge into the coming day as music
glancing off the swirl of the Milky Way.
As if it were always expected of us
to bloom again, we martyred ourselves
to nectariferous nourishment of insect hordes,
among them hungry monarchs,
whose females transform themselves
from caterpillars bursting from cocoons
as living art, to pollinate us and lay eggs
only on our tender shoots
in return for our sacrifice.
On the wing, monarchs
dream with us

of being together again,
one species giving
another immortality,
repeating a process
so lovely and
oblong.

This Light of Home

The road home sometimes drifts to a place off-grid
    where quince and forsythia line cinder paths,

a green hand pump draws well water, horsehair
    in plastered paper covers walls, an outhouse

stands in lilacs; where a furnace in a hand-dug basement
    burns coal, and smoke settles over the pines.

A place where mason jars of golden peaches
    with rugged red centers age in an earthen cellar.

A bed covered in goose down, pillows of feather tick
    clouds. A washboard leans on a steel tub.

From a high window, white curtains billow in sunshine.
    Come nightfall, the book on a table. A candle

dances shadows on the wall. The flicker
    of a fragile pulse of light—

IV.

A Talk with the Road to Nowhere

After decades of traveling away, on one particular morning I was drawn back off-grid, to the winding country road twisting through the tough hills and blind turns of land where I was born. My intention: to examine the tangled ball of neurons in my brain that had become worn, braided into the road. I knew that in one direction, away, the road led to everywhere else; in the other, to nowhere—a sooty coal town of forty row houses. This was the end I was unsure of today, the road's beginning. What was really there?

As the car's tires rolled off the main highway onto my road, they fell into its grooves as though they'd never been away. The road recognized the sound and feel of the tires crunching red-dog gravel as if they were my young legs jogging there once again. When the window rolled down, I knew it was the road trying to help. The breeze carried the lavender scent of wild alfalfa, and I remembered that the road was the way in and out of my heritage.

Along with the fragrance of alfalfa blooming, something else told me I was welcome as I had been so many times before: light bent the trees as it touched my road. Through this slant of light, I could see my old yellow school bus, the one that so often carried me home, rusting in trees along the road, the bus now the color of chain smoking, nicotine-stained fingers. I saw I.V. poles, plastic bags of crystalloid, hypodermic needles and syringes protruding from broken windows as if the bus was an overstuffed dumpster, the family chemotherapy garbage bin. I remembered all the trips my road and I took to the hospitals, the chemo sessions for grandparents, Elsie and Russell, Vera and Mike, then finally my parents, Helen and Don. Yes, that was it. No one left in the family for chemo. I realized the road had become my chemotherapy friend, traveling back and forth to the hospitals, then to the funeral parlors, the friend I never wanted to see again.

During those times, my road would talk, try to soothe me, but today I could feel the tangled mess of neurons untie themselves in my brain as I sidled up to my road to nowhere, deciding this time I should be the one to speak, to comfort the road. I leaned onto the shoulder of my road. As I did, the cottonwoods and sycamores leaned in, as if instructed by light, toward the two of us, my road and me, just as they had years before when the road was doing the comforting. My voice softened, faded. All it could muster was a whisper the trees, my road, and I understood. It was enough, what all of us needed to hear.

Empty Chair

Forgotten,   pulled   from the heap
                    of outcasts,
                fading in sunlight,
I   was revived,   sanded,   varnished,
    stood up straight,   refurbished,   to tell
                    the story.
No other artifacts   exist: no paintings,
    books,   clay pots,   silver platters,   not even
                    a poem.
I will remember   the story   for you,
        the times of   child labor,   scrip,
            company stores,   feed-sack dresses,
            babushkas,   John L. Lewis,
            AFL-CIO,   one-room schoolhouses,
            red dog gravel,   slag heaps,
                twilight league baseball,
            coal tipples,   blackdamp,
                    mine explosions.
I   know it all.   Many of you   once sat,
    leaned on me   singing   Christmas carols,
            playing pinochle,   swilling port.
    To go away   was everyone's   dream—
vanish   from this   obscure   sooty   town,
        used up   in the coal fields.   As
            I   sit   alone,
                coated in dust,   still
    I believe   there's   something
                    rewarding
to be here   without you,   cloaked
                in anonymity,
            covered up   in the sun.

House Where Shep Waited

Pete Garek's house looks down at the two
visitors walking together—old shriveled woman

in a feed-sack dress, followed by
husky Kid, wearing his same blue shirt.

The house eyes their shoes scraping the earth's
cinder path that keeps getting longer

each time they travel here. *Look up at me,*
the house demands! *Look up at the mirage*

on my porch! I am vacant now. Old Shep
no longer waits, lying beside the empty chair

for his lost Midway master to come home
from his shift at Willow Grove Mine.

Shep's vigil lasted years. The house waited
beyond its days of standing into the time

when it was torn down and given back.
Finally, the collie was pried from the arms

in the house, carried down the path, and he, too,
given back.

Voices in the Fluvial Fog

In heavy fog and rain that night, I knew from your voices
          I would not be coming back to stay.
Even my suitcase sighed on the sidewalk when Dad set it down,
          telling me this was it.
An empty bus hugged the road to the station just the other side
          of the Ohio, in Wheeling,
and took me away to a room at an airport where I was sworn in
          and sworn at,
uniformed and regimented. Flown away from everything
          I knew and loved,
all because of a war no one understood or wanted, I began
          to think about the gravity
in your voices that night.

I managed to return, but the two of you had already gone.
          I searched for sign of you
in a yard turned to stone: all I found were voices in the fluvial
          fog that had no pulse.
Thinking I could uncover your faces in the voices, I reached out
          to touch you, even called your names—

Last Man Out

Will the last man leaving Belmont County please turn out the lights
was spray-painted in cursive on the side of a rusted railroad
bridge over the highway leading out on State Route 9

Only one person lingered: the man whose job it was to turn out
      the lights
   so that greed could sleep.
Waiting until the strip-mined land was pronounced dead, buried
      under itself
   to sleep forever,
the last man out of Belmont County heard a voice that caused him to
      turn back.
   What he saw made him ill.
Orange water seeped from deserted mine shafts and slag heaps,
      earth's sulfur
   pouring into streams feeding Wheeling Creek.
Ponds of it filled deep holes with highwalls, covering slabs of
      unearthed rock
   and mud randomly strewn.
No clean water to drink—they didn't think it would ever come
      to this.
   The last man out hastily buried the final meadowlark,
then carried out the canary's empty cage, soon to be moved
      to another place
   yet untouched.

As he walked away from his home a second time, again
      the voice pleaded
   with him: *please turn out the lights.*

When he did, a slag heap spontaneously ignited as if someone
        had thrown
    a match into gasoline vapors.
The last man walking out looked into the eyes of fire to see the faces
    of all the others who had left before him,
one of whom was a poet who spoke these words out of the fire:

> *Given help and time enough, the land will heal.*
> *Its scars green, and the meadowlarks return.*
> *Let it now lie to rest awhile. When the land awakens,*
> *it will welcome you back, offer you its precious water,*
> *clean and sweet, sacred and pure.*
> *Be kind to the land and love it; in return the land*
> *will nourish and love you. This polite coexistence*
> *is the only way you can live with each other.*
> *Let yourself become the land, and the land become you.*

The last man out knew from looking into the eyes of fire
        that the voice
    he heard was the voice of God, the voice of the land.
He understood now what Robert Frost meant by his words *the land*
        was ours
    before we were the land's.
He knew he would return when the land called him back. The last
        man out
    felt forgiven.

A Broken Song for the Willow Grove Mine Disaster

A broken song for the Willow Grove Mine Disaster
        is forgotten until a tremor
shudders the ground. One clear morning each March,
        at precisely the eleventh hour,
a reminder radiates from the 22 South tunnel. Something
        trembles from below,
disturbs a cardinal. Momentarily off balance, his song
        of solitary notes is broken
as he clutches a barren limb in a cold orchard
        of bending apple trees
on the hill above Willow Grove.

The comfort of daybreak's cover of snow, a soft
        understanding in slanted rays of sun
of a world purely golden only at this given hour
        in winter light.
Shadows, still, of men in hard hats, colors encrypted in snow,
        blend with moving shadows.
One pastel, a young woman, walks lively through the quiet
        to a parked vehicle.
She feels something distant, pauses for the tremor.
        Unaware of the tunnel
and for no good reason, she looks instinctively upward
        through that ectoplasmic flash
from a fleeting trance to stare briefly into the golden light.

Then she straps her young son into his car seat almost identical
          to her unmet uncle
cinching the safety buckle on his miner's belt. But before
          she starts the engine to go,
looks upward once more from the shadows to the sky,
          pausing without ever knowing why.
The cardinal regains his balance on the limb and resumes
          his broken song.

Miscount

Only a small crowd had gathered. Almost
no one would remember that far back, now.

The speaker was the grandson of one of the men
being honored. He may have even looked

like his grandfather in one of those antique
oval-shaped pictures common in their day,

and stooped at the shoulders too, and
mustachioed like a Czech laborer sitting

in a dark corner at a local bar nursing a pilsner
after work, black grime ground-in deep under his

fingernails. And the worker might have even cleared
his throat identical to the way his grandson did

today at the podium, except he would be clearing it
of coal dust rather than nerves. He might have

confidentially spoken out to a friend seated across
from him in the dim light of the bar: *Annie will have*

our second child in the fall. We'd like a son this time,
but another daughter would be nice too.

In the back of the crowd at the ceremony, beneath
the blossoming apple trees, stood an old woman.

When the speaker read the names of the seventy-two
miners killed at Willow Grove, she turned to friends

beside her, saying: *my grandson is mistaken.*
There were seventy-three. After the explosion,

I lost one, a son, to be named John, who would
have been a coal miner, too. He should be counted.

End of the Road

Pulling all that was left from before and promises for what would be,
      heavy-footed oxen and iron-rimmed-wheeled wagons

      long ago crushed gray cinder and sandstone on Zane's Trace.
      Now a byroad, the trail wanders

      through the weary coal town of Midway.
      After crossing the shallows

of a wide Ohio creek, the road furrows in mud, climbs uphill
      from the bottomland,

meanders past a strategic springhouse welcome to both livestock
      and pioneer, then rests

      at the Stone House Inn, brown and thick like an overcoat
      on a blustery day.

      In the afterimage of the moving light they follow,
      a brimming trough of water

awaits travelers at the entry. Fresh water, shady cool and dripping
      wet from lathered horses' mouths,

      is as treasured today as it was in those early days
of settling America. Pioneers filled dry wooden barrels,

carried only enough on their Conestoga wagons to get them over
      the horizon to the end of the road

      where it falls from one world into the next.

The Miners' Sentinel in a Cage

Sing, yellow bird, in clean air.
Sentinel in a cage,
you lived in peril. A miner
carried you into his tunnel
to warn him of whitedamp,
firedamp and blackdamp
lurking in the deep hole.
He knew if you stopped
singing, began to sway
on your perch, he must leave,
before you flutter and fall
to the bottom of the cage.
Sing, canary, sing
your sweet song.
The faint air that once
brought you down
is gone, no longer
your responsibility.
Stay steady on your perch.
Now, there is no need
to return to that crude
and fragile place
you once guarded
as you breathed
beneath the world
in darkness.

The Letter Never Written

perhaps should have begun: *"Dear Mrs. Roosevelt,*
    Why did you defy superstition and take the tour

of Willow Grove, knowing it was considered bad luck
    for a woman even to set foot in a coal mine?

I understand it was good for publicity. We all
    saw the photograph of you in your hard hat

in the newspaper, its caption relating how safe
    the mine was, how clean and non-gassy

you found it to be. Well, you know what happened.
    My Johnny and so many others didn't come home

from their shift that day of the gaseous explosion
    in the 22 South-section tunnel. What do I do,

Eleanor? I'm only twenty-four. There's not much
    left for me in these hills now. Any advice?

Respectfully, Marjorie Graham Sklenicka.
    Snow carpeted the ground, covering

footprints entering the great hole. There is
    something to be said for the silence of snow.

In the aftermath, no trace of the mine exists, its face
    permanently sealed. Shrubs and other flora bloom

in springtime over the opening as apple blossoms fall
from trees onto Appalachian foothills far above

the 22 South tunnel, cloaking the ground with white
petals. Choirs of canaries sing in their branches.

Beads of Water Forming

Standing on the corner of the porch at the funeral home, I listen to droplets of water dripping above me. Drip . . . drip—water healing itself, small beads forming at the edge of spouting long after the storm. Watching one bead after the other assemble, I try to decide which road to take back home: the lighted highway or the old way through the dark, the back road that seems longer each time I travel there, but feels so comforting.

Inside the parlor lies my cousin, the one I never knew. I came to pay last respects and to see if anyone in the family would talk about Willow Grove. This cousin was the son of one of two uncles who did not survive the explosion—my father's uncles. I'd spoken to my cousin's sister, Constance Grimes, who didn't seem to want to remember those times, telling me she was only six when the mine cave-in occurred.

She did say it deeply affected her mother, Clara, when her father, Cecil, didn't come home from his shift that day in March when new spring snow lightly covered the ground. She said Clara sat on the porch swing for days, staring at the path, waiting for Cecil to walk back up. Constance said it affected her mind. After the incident, Clara either talked far too much or not at all. There was no in between, no safety net or cradle for her words. Even in old age, she'd sit on the porch, staring down the quiet path.

I look up from the porch of the funeral home to the bottom of the rain spouting above me to see another bead of water form and feel I should place the silence of my hands together to cradle it, before it falls onto the stone below and splatters.

Willow Grove Mine: Before I Was Done Talking

They shut me up,   sealed   my   mouth
            before
I was done talking,   but   hear
me,   listen to the water dripping
            inside
me,   the tinlike tinkling of wives
            of hollow miners
                lightly tapping spoons
                    on empty dinner buckets
as they stand
    in cold rain   waiting.
                I grumble to myself
                    deep down
in the tunnel
        of my throat,
making those
weak   gravelly   calls
        no one hears.
My ribs

                heave.

Beads
of
sweat
form   on untouchable   parts
of my body   and drip
    from petrified timbers
        like blood.

Drops of me

                                                   tumble

into pools

                      of muddy liquid   to mix

with sulfur and coal   until

                    I   scream   red,

cut   through fog   and smoke

                                              only

to hear myself   ricochet

                   off columns

of shale and rock.   My voice
trips   over   itself,
stumbles
   down
        the mine shaft,
         blindly
knifing,   knifing,   knifing
its   way   through   afterdamp,
        crying out
for an exit,
    a secret passage to air.

About the Author

Jonathan Graham was born along the Ohio River in Martins Ferry, breathed air that chugged from smokestacks at Wheeling Steel and grew up not far from there in an ethnic enclave of immigrant Slovak coal miners. Drafted into the military and serving first as a medic, then later in aviation, he went on to study poetry as a graduate student of American Literature/Creative Writing and medicine, becoming an Emergency Physician. Jon resides on a farm/sanctuary near the village of Zoar in the hilly woodlands of East Central Ohio.